The Year
of My
Miraculous
Reappearance

The Year of My Miraculous Reappearance

CATHERINE RYAN HYDE

ALFRED A. KNOPF

New York

THIS IS A BORZOI BOOK PUBLISHED BY ALFRED A. KNOPF

www.randomhouse.com/teens

Educators and librarians, for a variety of teaching tools, visit us at
www.randomhouse.com/teachers

Library of Congress Cataloging-in-Publication Data
Hyde, Catherine Ryan.
The year of my miraculous reappearance / Catherine Ryan Hyde. — 1st ed.
p. cm.
SUMMARY: Thirteen-year-old Cynnie has had to deal with her mother's alcoholism and stream of boyfriends all her life, but when her grandparents take custody of her brother, who has Down syndrome, Cynnie becomes self-destructive and winds up in court-mandated Alcoholics Anonymous meetings.
ISBN 978-0-375-83257-4 (trade) — ISBN 978-0-375-93257-1 (lib. bdg.)
[1. Alcoholism—Fiction. 2. Emotional problems—Fiction. 3. Brothers and sisters—Fiction. 4. Down syndrome—Fiction. 5. People with mental disabilities—Fiction. 6. Self-actualization (Psychology)—Fiction. 7. Alcoholics Anonymous—Fiction.] I. Title.
PZ7.H96759Yea 2007
[Fic]—dc22
2006029194

Printed in the United States of America

March 2007

10 9 8 7 6 5 4 3 2 1

First Edition

For my "tag team sponsors,"
Jane and Barbara

CHAPTER 1

The Revolving Door of
My Mom's Love Life

One night Mom got bad drunk because she'd had a fight with Harvey. Her latest boyfriend. I didn't know what he'd done to her, but I knew it must've been bad. I hated all her boyfriends, but Harvey was worse. I think he was rotten to her. I'm not exactly sure of the details. I mean, I'm not sure rotten exactly *how*. But I still think he was.

I was lying awake, which was not so very unusual in itself, and I smelled smoke. When I got out to the living room she'd set the couch on fire with her cigarette. I got there just as the first little flame shot up. I ran some water in a pot and threw it on the fire. It splashed all over her face and she came around, and boy, was she pissed.

So I said, "Hey, what was I supposed to do? You set the goddamn couch on fire."

She slapped me. She used all kinds of cuss words, and normally she didn't care if I did, too, but I had to leave God out of it.

She looked kind of pathetic, slumping there all wet with that damp cigarette butt in her hand. She had a new perm, and I think she thought it looked great, but it always ended up flat in some strange ways where she'd been lying on it. She'd gained a lot of weight and she was wearing one of those mint green polyester things that made her look like a pale avocado.

She must have caught that in my eyes but she didn't seem to want to fight back against it. Lately she seemed to get into being pathetic, like it had some value she was ready to cash in. It's like she was practicing, trying to get really good at it.

She started to cry again, and Bill started to cry, we could hear him back in my room. She looked in that direction, almost like she'd get up and go to him, but the drunk sag took over and she slumped down further.

"Maybe he'd be better off," she said. Real quiet.

"Maybe he'd be better off if what?" When Mom was drunk she had a bad habit of picking up in the middle of a conversation she'd forgotten to start.

"See if you can get him back to sleep, would you, Cynnie? It's so hard."

"What is?"

"You know. To take care of him."

"You *don't* take care of him. *I* do." And I went back to my room, or I should say Bill's and my room. He was standing

2

up in his crib, holding the rail, saying my name. Well, sort of. Cynnie, that's what everybody called me. Bill called me Thynnie, because his tongue was thick, from the Down's Syndrome, and that was the best he could do. And it sounded okay to me, the way he said it.

A lot of people thought Bill wasn't very cute. Maybe because his face was kind of puffy and he never closed his mouth. I think they didn't look at him right. He had the biggest, sweetest brown eyes, and right that minute he had the biggest tears rolling down his face.

"Thynnie," he said again, and bounced up and down a little in the crib, which was his way of telling me that what he couldn't say was very important. Bill was three years old but he still had to be in a crib because he was still a baby in his head. I'm not sure why everybody thought that was such a tragedy. I mean, people like babies, right? I know I do.

I whistled a little tune for him. I whistled the French national anthem, because the teacher made us sing it in French class so much I still had it stuck in my head.

When I'd finished a line he sang it back to me. Not with words, but the way people do when they forgot the words. And he bounced a little on every note. It was not my imagination that Bill could do that. Just because he wouldn't do it in front of anybody else didn't mean I was making it up.

I picked him up when he reached his arms out, and he buried his face in my neck and kept saying something. I couldn't make it out, but I knew for sure it was "Thynnie" because that's the only word Bill knew how to say.

He knew I was upset. I could never fool Bill.

3

He pointed to the living room. He always liked to watch TV with me. It seemed to soothe him. I carried him down the hall—no easy task, he was pretty darn big—and snuck a look around the corner. Mom wasn't around. She must have gone to bed. Good.

I turned on Jay Leno, because it didn't matter to Bill what we watched.

We sat on the couch together, way at the end to avoid the wet burned spot, and I put my arms around him, and he put his head on my shoulder. Every time I looked down, he was looking up at me.

I kept saying, "It's okay, Bill. Everything is going to be okay."

But nothing felt okay. And I could never fool Bill.

Kiki—that's our older sister—she said Bill's "profoundly retarded." She said that's a tragic thing. She's all grown up and moved away from home, so she's my authority on everything. Except Bill. I had this theory about Bill. I didn't exactly ask what "profoundly retarded" means, but I know when you say something profound you're being very deep and meaningful, so I figured that's why Bill knows so much, like whether I'm sad or scared or upset.

After a while he fell asleep with his head on my shoulder and I put him back to bed. I couldn't sleep with the smell of smoke to remind me, so I went outside and climbed up into my tree.

I had a branch that I lay on like a momma lion. I saw one in a film once at school, lying on a big limb, straddling it, all four legs hanging down. I could do that. Only, Momma Lion had a tail that twitched, while the rest of her looked plenty relaxed. If I'd had a tail, I think it would have hung down like the rest of me. I wasn't feeling all that twitchy.

With my cheek on that cool bare wood I could keep one eye on the house without feeling like I was any part of it. Either no one caught on to where I was, or more likely, they didn't care to look. I mean, the less commotion in that house, the better.

A few days later I found the pocketknife lying on the coffee table. Right away I knew it was something I wanted, smooth and valuable-looking, with a carved bone handle. It was Harvey's, which is part of why I took it. Payback, which he deserved. In general. I stuck it in my pocket and slipped out the back door and climbed up into my tree and carved a smooth spot for my cheek. I felt good, like I'd won something. Like I had something worth having.

After a while I could hear Mom and Harvey start to fight, but that was nothing special. I had no reason to think it had anything to do with me.

A minute later they came spilling out onto the back patio. From that angle I could see the way Harvey combed little strands of hair over his bald spot. He looked up into the tree at me, and he'd never had quite that look on his face. It made me squirm a little inside. I looked at the places on the house where the paint had peeled off to bare wood, just to have someplace to look. Someone should have told him to leave me alone when I'm in my tree. Harvey didn't even know the rules. Everybody should know the rules.

"Cynthia, Harvey says his pocketknife is gone. Have you seen it?"

Normally I would have kicked at being called Cynthia, but for the moment I thought I'd play my cards real carefully. "Um. What did it look like?"

"You know damn well what it looks like," he called up at me. "Now give it back, you little sneak thief."

I just smiled at him.

Mom punched him on the arm, hard enough to make him grunt. She was wearing that ratty old tan robe that made her hips look lumpy. "Harvey thinks you took it, dear. I told him you never would."

"Why would he think that?" Pure stall tactic. I knew why he would think that. It's because I was thirteen. Any loose crime lands on you when you're thirteen. And usually sticks.

"Because nobody else could have," he said. "Because your mom was with me the whole time and nobody else in this house is even smart enough to steal."

For a split second I thought of Rocky the Flying Squirrel, and I wondered whether I could leap on Harvey, knock the wind out of him, and make him pay for saying something mean about Bill. But the cement patio all around him looked pretty hard, and I didn't feel like Rocky. I felt kind of shaky and small.

Mom turned on him, pushing these strands of frizzy hair

out of her face, but they kept falling back again. "Now, Harvey, I told you the girl didn't take it, she said she didn't, that's the end of it."

"I didn't hear her say she didn't."

The knife felt bulky in my pocket and pressed into my leg. "I didn't take it."

Harvey turned on my mom, and his face looked like a kid who can't get his way. "You always side with her. You never listen to me—you take her side every time."

Mom pulled herself up to her full five feet nothing, tugged her robe around herself, and told him to get out. "You heard me, Harv. Pack what you got lying around and git."

He stared at her for a second. Then he said something too quiet for me to hear, but I could see it. I could see it hit Mom like a handful of stones, knocking her back a step with the force. Then he disappeared into the house. Mom just stood there, blinking. I'm not sure why she made me think of a turtle on its back.

"What'd he say, Mom?"

She ran inside, crying.

A few minutes later Harvey stomped out with a bunch of shirts over his shoulder, and a brown bag. His Chevy spewed all kinds of bad-smelling smoke when he revved it up. He always had to run it kind of high, to keep it from stalling, but this might have been more. This might have been to make a point.

When he disappeared around the corner I called something after him. I said, "Get lost, jerk." And then, after I'd had a little more time to think, I said, "It's about time you got lost. Loser. What a loser."

I scrambled down and went back inside. Just to make sure Bill was okay. I looked at the clock and it was eleven in the morning. Mom was pouring her first drink.

"What did Harvey say to you, Mom?"

She slugged down half the glass of gin and poured again. "It doesn't matter."

"Matters to me."

"Okay, you want to know?" The volume backed me up against the kitchen counter. I hadn't been set to expect it. "Fine, I'll tell you. He said between my thief daughter and my retarded son, it's no wonder I can't hang on to a man." In the silence that followed I watched the way her mascara puddled up in the wet spots under her eyes. She sniffled and said, "Okay. Now are you happy?"

I said, "No, I don't think 'happy' is quite the word that jumps to mind."

In fact, it's a funny thing about the word "happy." It's just a word I've heard people say. I never really knew what they meant by it at all.

I had some compadres to hang out in my tree with me. At least I thought they were my compadres. Richie, and Snake, whose real name was Morris. Richie was a year younger than me, Snake was one older.

We'd carve guns out of dry wood and play bandit games in the little aisles between the neighbors' garages. We knew we were too old for that junk but we did it anyway. They were just worthless bits of yard that nobody used, but it sure pissed people off to see kids in there.

The girls in the neighborhood were pretty rough on me. Called me Tarzan Girl and said I was uncivilized. But, you know, consider the source. Still, I took off when I saw them coming.

Richie said, "They suck, anyway."

Snake said, "I don't get why they say 'Tarzan' like it's not a good thing."

So, anyway, I figured they were my friends.

When we got bored of everything else we built a tree house up there. In my spot. Just the three of us.

When Zack showed up—Zack, that was Harvey's replacement in the revolving door of my mom's love life—he wanted to help. First thing. He almost climbed right up in the tree with us, because he said we didn't look like we were doing so good. We weren't. But it was a rule—no grown-ups allowed in that tree. Kids only.

Zack sat on the back stoop and popped a couple of beers and stared up at us. He looked skinny and strange to me, like somebody I'd never met before, even though he'd been hanging around for a few days. Still, they never lasted long, so no point to get attached. It's like naming a cat you don't get to keep.

It was just a little platform when we were done, and pretty rickety at that. It rocked when you walked over to the right-hand side. It had an egg-shaped hole in the middle that Snake cut with his father's keyhole saw, and stairs made of two-by-fours nailed to the trunk like ladder steps, so you could stick your head right up through the hole as you climbed.

I called down to Zack. I said, "Any grown-up who sticks his head up through this hole might get it whacked." I held up a leftover two-by-four to drive the point home.

He laughed and gave a little salute. Then Mom came out and told me to get down and get in the house, pronto.

As soon as I did, I got slapped for talking to her boyfriend like that.

"Boyfriend," I said. "Ha! Is that what we call them now."

I could see by her face that I'd gone way too far.

She came charging at me like something out of a nature film on National Geographic. I thought I was dead. Before she could get to me, Zack grabbed her around the waist and told me to go to my room while she cooled out. She broke his hold and stomped out of the house. I smelled another shopping spree. Not a pleasant odor.

I looked at Zack and he looked at me. Probably this was the part where I was supposed to say, "Oh, thank you, oh, aren't you cool," which pissed me off.

I said, "This is all *your* fault. Everything was fine before *you* got here." Which was a total lie.

"I was only trying to help," he said.

Then I felt kind of bad, because he didn't even get snotty with me.

When I got back to the tree house Richie and Snake had wimped out and gone home. They never came in my house.

Never. No one in their right mind would. I didn't even blame them. I climbed down and went inside.

Zack was nowhere around but Kiki was over, standing in the living room, flipping around on the TV channels by remote control. "Where's Mom?" she asked.

"I'm guessing out on another shopping spree."

"God help us all."

Kiki could say that, even if Mom had been here, because she was a very serious Christian. She really meant it when she talked about God, with no disrespect.

"What's wrong with your own TV at your own apartment?"

"I must've forgot to pay my cable bill. Come on, Cynnie, it's my best soap."

"Yeah. Whatever." I knew it must've been something. Kiki steers a mile around anything to do with this family if she can help it.

"Did you know Nanny and Grampop were coming?"

Something about that question got my stomach's attention. It was just one of those things that never happens, that has no call to happen suddenly, just out of nowhere.

"Why?"

"I dunno. Why not?"

"Like, when do Nanny and Grampop drive all the way from Redlands to see us?"

"Well, like, never, I guess. Mom called them weeks ago and asked them to come. I think it has something to do with Bill."

Just then Bill started to cry, because even from his playpen on the patio I swear that kid knows a lot. I carried him into the living room. When Kiki looked at him she said the same thing she always said. "Pray for that boy's soul, Cynnie."

I never told Kiki the truth, that I was afraid to pray. I figured, once I got started, then God would know where I was.

That night I lay in bed in the dark, whistling a little tune to Bill. I think it was "I've Been Working on the Railroad."

Listening to Bill sing back to me.

And I realized then that a momma lion protects her young. She doesn't sit back and let anybody take anything away from her.

CHAPTER 2

Zack the Brave and Stupid

I lit candles on the table, so we could halfway see what we were eating, except it was Mom's hamburger casserole, so maybe the less seen the better.

Zack came in late with gallon bottles of water, so we'd have something to drink. This was all good news if it meant I didn't have to do the dishes or take a bath.

I jabbed my hamburger stuff with a fork. Like it would be that easy to kill it. "Why are Nanny and Grampop coming?"

Usually I could tell a lot by Mom's eyes on a question like that, but only if she'd paid the light bill.

"To visit, honey, why else? Won't it be nice to see them?"

"Yeah. Swell." It was snotty, the way I said it. But she

pretended not to notice. I wished she'd call me on it. I wanted a fight.

I tore off a piece of bread and gave it to Bill to keep him busy until I was done and I could help him eat. Actually, he could eat fine, only not with forks and spoons. I figured that was nature's way of telling us to cut out the middleman. Mom did not agree.

Zack said, "Hey, tomorrow morning, Rita, I was thinking I'd go down to the utilities and get everything back on. You know, before your parents come."

The room got real quiet. Hard to believe you could make that much quiet just by sucking out all the noise.

"If it was that easy, Zack, don't you think I would have? What did you think you would use for money?"

Whoa. The glacier age was back.

"Well," he said, "I got a little put by."

Mom patted her mouth with the edge of her napkin and folded it up before she set it on the table. None of this was a good sign. "I am not a charity case, Zackary, and my feelings for you are not for sale."

"Honey, I never meant—"

"Drop it, Zack. Butt out."

"Hey," I said, half standing with my legs bumping under the table. "Don't you talk that way to Zack!"

I looked around and everybody was staring at me. Even Bill. I was hoping nobody would ask me why I did that. I was as surprised as anybody. More. I'd gotten caught acting like I liked Zack or something. I didn't like Zack. Did I? Anyway, even if I didn't, he was only trying to help. She could at least have been nice about it.

Mom excused herself from the table, saying she'd lost her appetite. I started feeding Bill, but it wasn't easy. Even Bill didn't like Mom's hamburger casserole, and he's easy to please.

"So, Zack, what do you know about this Nanny and Grampop thing?"

"Well, I think your mom's feeling snowed under taking care of two kids—"

"*I* take care of Bill. And myself."

"But you'll have to go back to school in the fall, and—"

"Forget it. They won't get him. I'm going to fight this thing. You'll see."

I got up and took Bill out of his high chair. Just as I stormed out of the room, Zack said, "Hey. G.I. Joe."

"What?" I yelled, spinning around.

"Before you break out the big artillery, you might try talking to them."

"Talking?"

"Yeah. Talking. Tell them how you feel about the kid. And tell your mom, while you're at it. Didn't you ever try talking to people when you had a problem? I mean, your grandparents are people, right? They'll listen."

I could feel a little sarcastic smile bend my mouth around. "I can see you never met Nanny and Grampop."

Just as I left the room I saw him take a second helping of hamburger casserole. It takes a special kind of brave or an extra kind of stupid to do that.

❖ ❖ ❖

Kiki was over, pretty much against her will, when Nanny and Grampop got in. And the lights were back on, because Zack was just brave or just stupid enough to think Mom wouldn't mind.

Nanny split my ears with that little squeal of hers. "Loretta! Look what a beautiful woman you are!" Kiki rolled her eyes at me.

Nanny will never call her Kiki. Never. Not until she dies. Not even if there's an afterlife. Kiki's birth certificate says Loretta, and Nanny is not big on change.

I just smiled as I watched Kiki get crushed. Even though I knew I was next. Nanny had this special hugging style, unless you were smart and you saw her coming. She always got one arm around behind your neck, and the next thing you knew she had you in a headlock that would bring Hulk Hogan to his knees.

Then she came at *me*. "Cynthia!" Too late to duck.

My face was pressed against all that perfect hair, which never once moved. I had a theory that Nanny's hair was removable, like Zack's motorcycle helmet. That she took it off and put it on the bedside table to sleep, and that she was like a conehead underneath. Nobody's real hair could be that tall, or that perfect, or that unmovable, or that red. It wasn't natural.

Meanwhile, Grampop did what he always did, hung back by the door. He always looked like he was ready for a fast getaway. Grampop only had one eyebrow but it was a doozy, running all the way across his face, knitted together like wiry gray wool in the middle, over his nose, which was also quite a show.

I said, "Nanny, I need to talk to you."

She said, "Of course, dear. We'll talk all weekend."

"No, I mean really, Nanny, it's important. It can't wait."

"Of course, honey, we'll get caught up on everything."

Then Nanny pulled Mom off into the kitchen and told her Zack was way too young for her, loud enough for everybody to hear.

Zack just offered to help Grampop bring in the bags.

I slipped out the back door and up into my tree. The patio door was open, and I could hear most of what was said, because everybody was shouting to be heard over everybody else.

I heard Nanny say, "What on earth happened to Cynthia? She was so anxious to visit, now she's gone."

Gone. Yeah. I wish.

Nanny never sleeps. She goes to bed early, but then she's up rattling around all night. She says the older you get the less sleep you need. But I didn't sleep half the night, either, so that made me feel old. I had something scared in my stomach.

I got up and sat at the kitchen table with Nanny, and she made me a cup of tea the way she used to when I was little, with sugar and milk. I liked that.

I said, "Are you taking Bill away?"

"Your mom thinks it's a good idea. She doesn't feel she can take care of him."

"*I* take care of Bill. And myself. And her."

"Well, that's too much for a girl your age."

"You can't take him, Nanny. You can't." I wanted to say why not. I wanted to say, He's all I've got. But it would've been so humiliating to cry in front of her.

I just kept stirring my tea, listening to the little *clink-clink* of the spoon on the cup. When other people do things like that it drives me crazy. Drumming fingers. Jiggling legs. I'd kill over less. She never answered, so I knew it was all decided.

I said, "It's not Bill's fault. She just thinks it's Bill's and my fault that her boyfriends don't stay. Because one idiot boyfriend told her that, and she was dumb enough to believe it. And lay off Zack, what do you care how old he is?" I was getting off the point but the detour felt good.

"Why, Cynthia, I—"

"Listen to me. Listen, Nanny. You never listen." She looked hurt. I never thought I could hurt Nanny, but then I felt bad that I had. I thought she was as unmovable as her hairdo. "Mom doesn't do anything around here. Zack just got the lights back on because Mom went shopping with the money to pay bills. She doesn't take care of me or Bill at all. She barely takes care of herself. It's pathetic. And she drinks way too much." Then I thought about Zack sitting on the steps popping beer-can tops, so I said, "Not that there's anything wrong with drinking. You just have to know when to stop. And she doesn't. At all. And another thing. Do you have any idea how many boyfriends she's had through here since last time you came?"

I could hear her breathing so clearly, big pull in, big sigh. "Well, if that's true, dear, it's all the more reason that Bill should be with us."

"What about *me*? *I* have to live with her."

"You're older, dear, and you don't have Bill's special needs."

"Nanny, you can't take Bill. You can't. Please. You have to help me. You have to talk to her. We all have to talk to her about taking some responsibility."

Nanny drank every bit of her tea without saying a word and put our cups in the sink. "No need to embarrass her in front of everybody. I'll talk to her privately in the morning."

In the morning the house was way too quiet. I found Nanny in the kitchen.

"Did you talk to Mom?"

"She's going to try. But it's all the more important that Bill come with us."

"When are you leaving?"

"Tomorrow morning."

Okay, I thought. Okay. Then Bill and I are leaving tonight.

I taught Bill how to hitchhike. We stood by the side of Highway 101 together, my big duffel bag lying in the dirt. I stuck my thumb out and he held his stuffed elephant in one hand and stuck his thumb out with the other. I had Harvey's knife in my front jeans pocket, to make me feel not so helpless.

I think it was about two in the morning. I'd never been out at two in the morning, so that was weird. Don't bad things happen when it's that late?

After a while we got a ride from a man in a big Lincoln, with uniforms hanging all neat and pressed on hangers in the back. He said he was a guard at the state prison, and he was going almost as far as Los Angeles, all but ninety miles of the way. He drove really fast. He'd get about an inch from the car in front and say it made him so mad when they went too slow that he wanted to bang right through them.

All of a sudden I got to feeling all helpless again, like something bad could happen, and then how would I take care of Bill? It was my job now, more than ever.

Then Bill started to cry, because he knew I was scared.

I said, "I think he has to go to the bathroom." Even though I knew he didn't. I just wanted to get out of that car.

The man stopped at a gas station, and we went around the back, where the bathrooms were, and over the little fence and down into a deep, brushy gully where we stayed until the man stopped calling and drove away.

L.A. was a good, big place to get lost, but I'd heard stories about it, too.

We hitched back toward town. I thought we'd stay at Kiki's for the night and then make a better plan.

The first car that came by was the sheriff's. I started walking the other way. I tried to slip down an off-ramp, but Bill didn't walk too fast, so I picked him up and tried to hurry without looking like I was running. I didn't look behind me until I saw his flashing lights. He was pulling us over. How can you pull someone over who doesn't have a car? But I stopped, because I figured I'd better.

That's when I realized the duffel bag went south without us, but just as well. It only made us look more like runaways.

He rolled down his window. "Evening, young lady."

"Yes, sir."

"Little late for you to be out. Who's your friend here?"

"This is my son."

"Do tell."

"Yes, sir, I'm older than I look, nineteen, and my son and I are trying to get home."

"Well, jump in the car and I'll take you there."

Bill and I got in the back. I was thinking about whether I was under arrest, and would it be a bad idea to ask. The sheriff leaned over the seat. He wasn't too old, and he had wavy black hair and a fluffy mustache. I kind of liked his eyes, though right at that moment I'd have been happy never to see them again.

"Got any I.D.?"

"I.D.? Uh. No, sir."

"Don't tell me you forgot your driver's license?"

"Driver's license?"

"Nineteen-year-old girl like you must have a license."

"No, sir. I mean, yes, sir. I forgot it. Like you said."

He leaned farther over the seat and he smelled like Old Spice aftershave. "Did you know it's against the law to run away from home?" My stomach got all iced and tingly. I didn't answer, even when I tried. "But let's give you the benefit of the doubt. You're on your way home, like you say. Where might that be?"

I gave him our address and he drove us home.

He walked up to the door with us and knocked, even though I tried everything I could think of to talk him out of it. The sun was up now, barely, and my mom came to the door in that ratty tan robe, with her hair all squished and little pillow lines in her face, and I was embarrassed for the sheriff to see her that way.

"These little strays belong to you?"

Mom's eyes got wide. "Did she do something wrong, officer?"

"Just headed out of town is all."

"Well, thank you very much for bringing her home. I'll take care of this."

He smiled at me before he left, and I was so convinced that he was an okay guy that I gave him a dirty look, like to say, Yeah. Thanks a lot.

It was almost five; it would be light soon. Nanny and Grampop would be up packing to go. Packing Bill. I had a talk with myself. I said, what kind of momma lion are you? You scared of a little old sheriff?

Truth is, I don't think I was scared, really. Because I don't think I really cared what happened. I mean, if Bill was going to be gone, it didn't matter. Nothing mattered.

It was more like I couldn't really move. I don't know quite

how to say this. Like I was a sailing ship and all of a sudden the wind stopped blowing. And all I could do was drift around on all that glassy water. Or maybe that sounds too nice. Maybe it was more like one of those awful dreams where you have to run to save your life, but you can't run. You just can't. Your arms and legs turn to lead, and that's it. Sitting duck.

Whatever it was, next thing I knew, it was morning. And we still weren't gone.

Nanny puttered around Bill's room, packing his clothes and a few toys. She almost left his elephant in the bottom of the crib. See, this is why they couldn't take him. How could Bill live with someone who didn't know the elephant was the very most important?

"I take care of Bill," I kept saying. If I'd said more, I'd have cried.

"Well, now you can have a childhood and not worry."

I kept trying to think of something to do. Wrestle her down or something. Instead I kept taking Bill's clothes out of the suitcase and putting them away again. Nanny would give me a look, then take the things out and put them back in the suitcase. I'd grab them again and put them back in Bill's dresser drawer.

"Stop that, Cynthia," Nanny said.

But I wouldn't stop. I was getting more and more upset. I was starting to throw things into drawers instead of just setting them down. I warned her. I warned her I wasn't letting them take Bill away.

She grabbed my arm, and I pulled it away so hard and so fast, I almost pulled her right over. So I guess it looked almost like I was trying to hit her or something, but I was only taking my arm back.

Then I saw Grampop standing in the doorway, and he yelled at me. He yelled, "Cynthia, you get out of this house if you can't behave!"

Something about that and about getting arrested, it made me feel tired and little, like no one was home inside, like nothing would do any good. Everything in the world was bigger than me. I never won and I felt like I never would. I went up to my tree house and cried where nobody could see.

After a while I heard Grampop calling, telling me to come say goodbye. At first I wasn't going to do it. I didn't want to see Bill's face in that car when they drove away. But then, when I heard the car start up, I climbed down and ran after them.

Grampop stopped the car, and Nanny got out and said, "There you are, Cynthia. We almost didn't get to say goodbye."

Bill was in his car seat in the back, half turned around to look at me, and he was talking. I could see his lips move, but I couldn't hear him, but I knew he was saying "Thynnie," because that's the only word Bill knew how to say. And I started to cry, right in front of everybody.

"Take *me*," I said. "I want to get out of here, too."

Nanny hugged me too hard and said somebody had to stay and help my mom, and I should be a big girl about it.

I said, "I want to live with you and Bill. Please?"

She got that look on her face, like when I hurt her feelings, and said it'd been hard enough to talk Grampop into taking Bill.

Then she kissed me on the cheek and drove away, and all the way down the driveway Bill's lips were still moving.

That night I couldn't get to sleep. My stomach was all twisty and full of needles. I tried to think what people do when they feel this bad. There had to be some way to make it stop. Even for a little while. I knew what my mom would do. She always drank at times like this. I would have tried anything to feel better by then. I'd thought about trying it lots of times before, but back then I didn't, because who would've taken care of Bill?

I borrowed a beer from the refrigerator and took it into bed with me. It tasted really nasty. I thought, how can anybody drink this junk? But by the time I was half done, things got a little fuzzy inside, which was good. Then I could see why Mom liked the stuff. I still felt bad, but in a muddy way. And the needles in my stomach were gone.

I finished the beer and lay there whistling a little tune. I don't remember which one. Just that nobody sang it back to me.

It was only me, whistling in the dark.

CHAPTER 3

Kid Trees

At first I hung out in the tree house by myself. I was in no mood for Richie and Snake. Then, even when I let them come up, I was still in no mood for them. They came up and hung blankets around the tree house to make it like a tent. For more privacy, you know? But that turned out to be too much of a good thing, because Snake, who was fourteen, started getting big ideas. I guess we'd made it *too* private a space.

All of a sudden he got this weird look on his face and said, "We could be doing it, you know. We're old enough."

Right in front of Richie, he said that. I couldn't believe it. I didn't know if he meant with each other or in general. But it was pretty much a "no" either way.

I said, "I've heard all about that. Nobody is old enough as far as I'm concerned."

He gave me this look like I was a big baby or something.

Even if I'd wanted to do it, which I didn't, I don't think Snake would have been the guy. He looked too much like a bulldog. He had this flattop that he thought was cool, and he was kind of chunky. As he squatted in that tree house, ragging on me about it, this little beam of light came through a hole in the blanket right over his head and made him look like he was wearing a halo, which just didn't fit.

Then he said, "Your mom and that Zack guy are doing it." He looked kind of weird and eager, like it was something he'd been dying to talk about.

I said, "Well, I'm not really so sure." I was, of course—I mean, it was pretty obvious—but I just didn't feel like going on about it.

Then Richie, the little squirt, the one who couldn't even keep his own nose clean, he said, "Your mom does it with everybody."

So I decked him.

I spun around and slammed him one, only not the way I wish. I wanted a nice roundhouse punch, but really I'd never thrown a punch in my life. I just gave him a shot to the nose with my elbow. It wasn't pretty but it worked. He stumbled backwards with blood squirting out of his nose, hit one of the hanging blankets, and took it down with him. All the way down he kept swinging his arms like he could get his balance, like there was still time not to fall.

I remember the sound he made when he landed.

I guess I was supposed to feel sorry about what I did, but I didn't feel much of anything. I looked at him lying down there and felt like he deserved it. I knew if I'd had it to do over, I'd have done it just like that again. Maybe thrown a cleaner punch. Some things are pretty much worth what you have to pay for them. Sometimes it's just worth it.

Snake came up into the tree house the next day. I'd been hanging out up there by myself since the whole Richie thing went down. This time I was in no mood for anybody, but I let Snake come up because I wanted to hear what was happening.

Snake had a big knot of bruise on the side of his head. I think he must've gotten in fights a lot, because it seemed like he had bruises most of the time. I never saw him fight, but then lots of things happen with people when you're not around to see.

He sat cross-legged on the boards. "You really messed him up," he said. "You broke his nose, and then he broke his arm when he fell."

"I bet he ratted me out, too."

"No. He told his parents he just fell. But he told a couple of the guys at school. So now the word is out. So now you're pretty much poison. I don't think anybody's gonna hang out with you now. Not even the guys."

I was liking people less and less, so I didn't take the news all that hard. "Fine," I said. "Who needs 'em?" It was kind of better, when you didn't even pretend to have friends. When you just made up your mind not to. It was easier.

28

We were quiet for a minute, thinking how life gets real dark and heavy all of a sudden, and then you go back and look for that moment when it changed, but it's too late to undo it.

At least, *I* was thinking that. I don't really know what Snake was thinking.

When I looked up he was staring at me. I could tell he wasn't mad or anything, but something about his face made my stomach feel weird. Just for a minute I thought I sort of liked him, because he looked at me like I was really there. I couldn't think of one other person who looked at me like I was really there.

I looked at his eyes and thought maybe I'd never really noticed how cool they were. Kind of light blue, clear, like ice.

"I'll still hang out with you," he said.

"But then you won't have any friends, either."

He looked down at the board floor. Shrugged. "Even so. I'll hang out here if you want."

"No," I said. "Don't do that just for me. Just wait. Things'll blow over. I'll be fine on my own."

He shrugged again. Then he got up and climbed down the ladder and disappeared. He never said anything, not even "bye."

What his problem was, I didn't know.

After a few weeks alone Zack came to my rescue. He took me for a ride on the back of his motorcycle, probably because he felt sorry for me.

He had on a black leather jacket, and that was cool, but it was the only thing about him that was, the way I had it pegged. Well, okay, his boots were cool. I wanted ones just like them, but I knew Mom would have a fit, because she thought I didn't dress enough like a girl. I mean, who would want to?

Anyway, I wouldn't hold on to Zack, because that's too creepy. It's not like I was his girlfriend or anything. I held that strap that goes across the seat, but there was nothing behind me to lean on, and when he put on the gas, I felt like I was going to blow right off the back.

And boy, could he put on the gas.

Once I got a peek at the speedometer and we were doing eighty-five. Just at that moment I think I might have understood what Mom saw in Zack. What Zack saw in Mom, now that's another story altogether.

He took me out the old reservoir road, and the leaves on the pavement did this little whoosh thing as we came by, kind of turned a spiral and ran away. When we came around curves the bike leaned over until I thought our knees would scrape the pavement. At first I was afraid to lean with him, because I thought the bike would dump right over, but it didn't, and I started to get into it. Scary, but cool.

Just for a minute I was ashamed of myself for feeling good. I'd been so careful not to lately. But then I decided Bill wouldn't mind.

I got to watch black and white cows hanging out in front yards and barns that looked like a good wind would take them down. Old combines and tractors rusting right where they had broken, and avocado trees, and persimmon trees, and the fence posts seemed to rush by like they were under their own steam.

Not that I hadn't seen all this before, but these things don't really come through the car window. Like that old saying about how things suffer in the translation.

All of a sudden I had this thought about perspective. But I'm not sure how to say it so it makes sense. Like, what if there was a farmer in the field and I could talk to him somehow, like by cell phone. And I said the fence posts were racing by and he said no, they were standing still. Wouldn't that be a stupid thing to argue about? But we do that all the time, argue with each other about what things are or what we think we see, and maybe that's the problem all along. Like we're not standing in the same place, or at least we're not moving at the same speed, so maybe it's all about perspective. I'm probably not explaining it right at all. I just decided that life was like a farmer standing in a field and a kid racing down the road on a Kawasaki, arguing about whether the fence posts are rushing by or standing still. Each thinking the other is crazy or blind or both, neither willing to give up until the other sees the light.

We got off by the reservoir, which was good, because my butt hurt. I wouldn't have said so. By that time I was thinking this Zack was a pretty cool guy, but then he took off his helmet and it was back to geek city. What do you expect of a guy who just got kicked out of the Air Force? I don't know what he did wrong, but it sure wasn't refusing to cut his hair. It was, like, a quarter-inch long, with little ridges where the helmet had squashed it down, and his face was sort of shiny. If he hadn't

31

been six foot four, he wouldn't have looked much older than me.

Actually, I think he was only about ten years older than me, which made him about the same age as Kiki. That was the age of the three kids in our family: twenty-three, thirteen, and three. Mom used to say, "Yeah, well, once every ten years whether I need one or not." Everybody thought that was funny. Except me.

Zack lit a cigarette.

I said, "Hey, don't I get one?" Richie used to let me have one of his cigarettes now and then. Back when I thought we were friends. I didn't expect Zack to be that cool, but it was worth a try.

"Aren't you too young?"

"Fine. Then I'll just get one later, from somebody else."

"Wouldn't your momma mind?"

"Only if you told her."

He looked at me kind of crosswise for a minute, but then he gave me one, like I was beginning to figure he would, because he wanted me to like him. He even lit it for me. I took a couple of drags and inhaled the first one to impress him. I knew better than to do that all the way down.

"So, how come you're such a tomboy?" he asked.

I'd gotten the question a lot, but I kept that to myself. "I don't know what you mean," I said.

"How come you always wear those baggy black sweatshirts and those jeans all ripped out in the knee?"

I shrugged and started skimming stones on the reservoir.

I never answered. He probably only asked because my mom was always squawking about it. I was wishing he'd get to the speech. He got to it soon enough.

"I know how you feel, Cynnie, but it might be the best thing for Bill—for everybody."

Yeah, sure, I thought. Just leave me out of your everybody. And while you're at it, leave Bill out of it, too. "I guess I'm taking my life in my hands, saying that to you." I just skipped stones. I didn't even tell him how much. I figured he knew. "I know it's a little hard for you to accept me," he said. "Me being so much younger than your mom and all." I shrugged and skipped another one. She'd done worse, I was thinking. I was dizzy from the cigarette but it wouldn't do to let on. "I know you don't like me," he said. I shrugged and let fire another stone. Good one. Five skips and then that nice little plunk. "But I love your mother very much."

I took a drag on the cigarette and looked him dead on. I didn't doubt him for a minute. "She won't let you." I'd been watching my mom real carefully, and I'd finally figured this out. She said she wanted love, but she made sure she never got any.

"Meaning what?"

"Mom doesn't want a man to be happy with. Because Mom doesn't want to be happy."

He screwed up his face and said, "That doesn't sound like something for a thirteen-year-old to say."

I said, "Well, I'm thirteen. And I just said it."

He laughed the way grown-ups do when they say they're laughing *with* you. Only I'm never laughing.

33

Then he pulled a flask out of his jacket pocket and took a snort of something.

"I'd take some of that," I said. I'm not exactly sure what "that" was. But on him it looked like a good idea, and I wanted to give it a try.

"Bad enough I gave you the cigarette."

I opened my mouth to try the old wheedle and whine, but he didn't even give me that much time.

"This one's not negotiable," he said.

That pissed me off a little, so I turned my back on him. Like only rocks existed in the universe.

"You know what it reminds me of," he said, "when I see you up in that tree?" I shrugged and braced for the worst. "It reminds me of a story I wrote in high school. Haven't thought about it for years, but I think about it all the time now. It was about these hordes of little kids who just sort of . . . packed up and split. The girls launched out to sea on boats, and the boys climbed up in trees. The Coast Guard went out looking for the girls but they were gone. And the fire department put ladders up in the trees but they were empty."

I dropped my cigarette and completely forgot to look cool. "Gone? Like, for good?" It seemed almost too good to be true, even in somebody's imagination.

"Yup. Forever. Teacher didn't like it, though."

"Figures."

"She said she didn't understand it. Where did I think these thousands of kids had gone? I said, 'Well, someplace that's really a whole different world. They just went somewhere different.' Know what she said?"

34

I shook my head in a way that must've looked stupid.

" 'What's wrong with *this* world?' "

"But she was kidding, though. Right?"

"Don't know. To this very day I haven't figured that out."

"She must have been kidding."

"She only gave me a C-plus."

I shrugged and skipped another stone, the spell broken. "Grown-ups," I said.

"Yeah. Grown-ups."

I held on to Zack on the way home.

Later that night I was sitting up in my tree house, to get away from the fighting. Mom had locked Zack out of the bedroom and he was pounding on the door and shouting. That went on for fifteen or twenty minutes. Then beautiful silence for an hour or so.

I saw Zack come out and sit on the back stoop. He looked up like he was trying to see if I was up there watching or not, but it was too dark to really see. All of a sudden I knew I'd been waiting and watching for exactly this, but I didn't know it until it happened. Isn't it weird that you can be thinking things and feeling things and not even know it?

I climbed down.

"Hey," Zack said when I sat on the porch next to him. He was acting like he wasn't still upset but I could tell he was. I could hear it in his voice, even just that one word.

I said, "Hey."

Then we sat like that in the dark for a while, and I knew I wanted to say something to him, but I couldn't figure what it was supposed to be. Once I even opened my mouth, thinking it would say itself as I went along, but nothing came out.

Zack was drinking a beer out of the bottle, a longneck. When he took out a cigarette I reached my hand out and he gave me one. And neither one of us even had to say a word.

The smoke felt hot and burny going down into my lungs, but I didn't mind.

"Do you still have that story somewhere?" I asked, and my voice sounded really jarring to me after all that quiet.

"What story?"

"The one about the kids who disappeared."

"Oh. That one. Oh, hell, that was so long ago. I've moved probably thirty times since then. And once when I was in jail my roommate threw out all my stuff." His words sounded squishy, not hard at the edges. Like my mom when she drinks too much.

I reached for his beer bottle and pulled it out of his hand. My hand brushed his just a little bit while I did it, but I didn't do that on purpose. I don't think. I didn't answer because I didn't want him to hear that it had been important. I just took a long swig of beer.

Zack said, "I had a feeling that story would mean something to you."

"How did you know?"

"Because we're alike, you and me."

Then, before I could even ask how, he got up and walked back into the kitchen. But I knew he was coming back, because he left half his beer, and a cigarette burning on the edge of the porch. I snagged another couple of gulps of his beer. All of a sudden I realized I could hear crickets. And that I'd been hearing them all along. Maybe I always heard them. Maybe that's why I never really heard them anymore.

Zack came back with two beers, with the tops already off, and handed one to me. The bottle was cold and wet and sweaty in my hand, and just for a split second I thought I liked being alive. I mean, it was okay. Maybe this is what people meant when they used that word. "Happy."

"How are we alike?" I said, even though I knew he was right.

"Because we're broken people," he said. "We walk and we talk and we act like we know what to do, but deep down we know it's different with us. That's why we do crazy shit sometimes. Make sure we feel alive. Like we're whole, just for a minute. You know?"

"Yeah," I said. "I know." I thought on that for a bit. "But I think the world is full of broken people. Way I see it, anyway. I look around and practically everybody I see is."

"Yeah, but they don't know it. We know what we are. They think they're okay."

I thought about my mom. Wondered if she thought she was okay.

We sat in the dark and the quiet a while longer, and the beer was making my muscles unkink. I was probably drinking it too fast, but I was thinking if I finished it right up he might get me another. I wondered if he was listening to the crickets, too.

"What makes you feel whole for just a minute?" I asked him.

"Driving my motorcycle really fast. A good beer buzz." He paused like he was thinking. Not like he was trying to think of another one. More like he was trying to decide whether to say it. "Love. What about you?"

"Bill," I said, and almost blew it by crying.

"Oh. Sorry." He got up to go. Like he thought the right thing to do was to leave me alone to feel this thing, and that was the last thing I wanted. But I couldn't think what to say to stop him.

He slid his unfinished beer over to me. "See you in the morning."

And I couldn't even say good night. I couldn't say anything.

After he left I picked up his beer instead of mine and put it up to my mouth, right where his mouth had just been. I wasn't that anxious to go back inside, so I just sat.

When I finally went to bed I found Zack out cold on the floor in front of my mom's bedroom door. Next to his head were two neat rows of beer bottles. Thirteen. I counted.

I think it was the next morning that I got it in my head about the pictures. I started looking around the house at all the pictures. There was Kiki as a little kid, and graduating high school. There was one of me on Trudy, my uncle Jim's horse, and a wedding picture of my mom and dad. A picture of my dad with a big bass he caught, about a month before he died.

But no Bill.

My mom was in the kitchen making coffee. Squinting, like her head hurt. Zack was already at work, I guess. Anyway, he was gone.

"Why are there no pictures of Bill?"

"We have pictures of Bill."

"Where?"

"Um . . . on the refrigerator."

"That's just a picture I drew of him."

"Well, that's a picture."

"I meant a photograph."

"Oh. Well, why doesn't a drawing count? It's such a nice picture."

"It is not. It sucks. And it doesn't count because you put it up on the refrigerator because you were proud of me for drawing it. Not because you're proud of Bill. It could've been a drawing of a tree for all you care."

She looked at me like I had asked her to do a complicated math problem in her head. I waited. But she just kept opening her mouth and not saying anything.

"Are you ashamed of him?"

"No! Of course not."

"Then why didn't you ever take his picture?"

"Well, honey, it's just that . . ." Another long wait. Another minute of my life I'd never get back.

"*What?* It's just *what*, Mom? Spit it out."

"Well, it's just that those are all special occasion pictures. You know. We took pictures of the family when one of us was doing something special."

"And Bill never did anything? Is that it?"

"You're blowing this all out of proportion," she said. You could see her make that shift in her head, where she decided to act defensive to make me go away.

"You're unbelievable," I said.

Then I went into the kitchen and took my drawing of Bill off the refrigerator. It wasn't really that good. I took it into the living room and tore it up right in front of her.

"There. Now we have no pictures of Bill. What are we going to do about it?"

She just rolled her eyes and lit a cigarette. She never answered. Like, what's new?

I threw the pieces up into the air, and we both watched them flutter down onto the rug like confetti. Then I went away, which I'm sure is what she'd wanted all along.

After school that day I wrote a letter to Nanny and Grampop. It said, "Please take a picture of Bill and send it to me. So I have something to remember him by."

Otherwise you could look around this house and think maybe he was just a dream I had. Maybe he really never existed at all.

The night after that Mom and Zack had a fight. A big one. And then, the next night, they had another.

I spent about six whole days up in that tree, alone, pretending I might wake up in a whole different world. And that's all it was, too. Pretending. All the time I knew it was stupid, and that I was too old for that junk, but something about it being Zack's idea made it seem a tiny bit less than impossible.

The night he left I woke up when his motorcycle kicked over. I climbed down fast, but he was out the driveway and headed down the street. I ran after him for almost two blocks, yelling his name as loud as I could, even though I knew he couldn't hear me.

My throat hurt and my lungs were ready to burst, and besides, the neighbors were turning on their porch lights and coming out to see. So I just waved my arms in case he looked in his rearview mirror, but I should have known he had no cause to look back. I kept thinking if I could get on the back of that bike, I could disappear with him. Forever. Then he turned a corner and he was gone.

When I got home I rousted Mom out of bed. "Where did Zack go?"

She said, "Don't you yell at me, young lady."

I didn't even know I'd been yelling. But I also didn't care. "I have to know, Mom. I have to know where he went, so I can write to him."

"I don't know," she said. "I don't know and I don't care, so get out of my room and let me get some sleep."

That pissed me off, that she talked to me like that. It pissed me off that she made Zack go. I guess really I'd been pissed at her ever since Bill got taken away. I guess I'd been sitting on this big ball of blaming her for everything. It's like I'd been afraid to even start with that. It was like a locked-up thing I was afraid to even open.

I took that ugly pottery lamp off the bedside table and

smashed it on the floor. Just for a split second I watched it start to fly apart, and then the room was dark. I waited. To see what she would do. Nothing. I couldn't even hear her moving.

I went to stomp out, but on the very first step I got a big sharp piece of pottery in my foot. I wanted to yell out, but I didn't. It'd be weak. Besides, it was my fault that crap was on the floor. I had no right to say ouch. I didn't *get* to cry.

I hobbled out into the kitchen and turned on the light, and pulled the piece of lamp out of my foot, and put on a Band-Aid so I wouldn't keep bleeding on the floor. I didn't clean up the blood that was already there. I went out to the living room and took a fresh, unopened bottle of her gin. Just as I got my hand around it, I looked up and saw her watching me.

I didn't even take my hand off it. I just stood there, staring her down. I was waiting for her to tell me to put it the hell back.

I said, "Well?" I waited. Nothing. "*Do* something." Geez. I mean, stop me. Or something. "Try being a mother for a change." She just turned her face away. I snorted at her. "You're pathetic," I said.

I took the bottle.

I took it back up in the tree house. This time, I told myself, I'm not coming down. I drank about a fifth of the gin. It made my arm and leg muscles all runny inside. I knew it was too much, but I wanted that. I wanted too much. I did it on purpose. It's not like I had Bill to look after. When he was home again I wouldn't get drunk anymore. But he was gone, so why should I care? I wanted to see if there was a line, and what was on the other side. And if it was anything like disappearing. And how long it could make me feel whole.

While I was doing that I saw her cart the pieces of lamp to the outside trash cans. She didn't even look mad. She just cleaned it up. She looked a little wobbly, though. Then she went inside, without even looking up at me.

Just as she was walking away, I thought I wanted to say something. I almost said something to her. Like maybe I was sorry for what I'd said before. Like maybe I went too far even for me. But I froze in it. I couldn't figure out which was worse, to do that and not say sorry, or to have to admit how bad I felt. They both felt so awful that I just froze and couldn't do anything at all.

After a while I saw the last light go off in the house.

Now, as far as the part about not coming down, I was wrong. I was pretty deep asleep, or passed out, and I guess I must have rolled over to the right-hand side, the rickety side, because I heard this crack, and I was flying through the air, still too much asleep to get the message.

I landed real hard on my left side and just lay there for a while. I was thinking, I know this means something, and in a minute I'll put my finger on what it is.

When I opened my eyes I figured out it was morning. The light felt like fire in my eyes. My tongue felt all thick and fuzzy and I wasn't sure if I would throw up right then or just very soon.

And to make matters worse, Snake was standing over me.

"You okay, Cynnie?"

"Maybe."

"Looks like we've got some repairs to do."

"I don't think so."

"What do you mean?"

I sat up carefully and wrapped my arms around my knees, and pressed my forehead between them, where it was dark, and closer to safe. I said, "I've been thinking a lot about this disappearing thing."

"Disappearing how? You mean like magic tricks?"

I said, "No. That's just it. I've decided there's no magic to it at all. I've decided I just have to get a lot more real about a lot of things."

"I don't read you."

I guess I didn't really expect him to. Because I'd never told him the beginning of the conversation. I hoped that didn't mean I was getting to be more like my mom.

I said, "Maybe the two of us ought to disappear."

"You mean, like, for real?"

"Yeah. Like, forever."

I opened my eyes just enough to see the look on his face. It was a mistake. The light almost made me sick. But his face was all open with surprise, like something wonderful and amazing had been led down the street in front of him. I sort of liked that about Snake. Some things actually made him happy, and he admitted it.

"You and me?"

"Why not?"

"Does this mean you're my girlfriend?"

Another wave of sickness, which may or may not have been related. I really hadn't bothered to think that part out. Or any of the rest of this, really.

"Snake, you think of a way to get me out of this town forever and I'm your girlfriend."

"Cool."

"There's a catch, though. We're taking Bill. Or no deal."

CHAPTER 4

Snake's Got It Worse than Me

Mom's new boyfriend was a real loser. He always sat too close to me on the couch, and he wouldn't stay out of the tree, even under threat of two-by-four. I tried to talk to Mom about it but she wouldn't believe me. She said I was just sore because Zack was gone, and that there was nothing she could do about that. So I spent a lot of time at Kiki's.

Kiki was hardly ever home anyway, or if she was, I'd watch her run around getting ready for work or a date. I liked to watch her put on her makeup. It was like the construction of a new building, from the ground up.

One day I told her I wanted to talk about boys.

"Ooooh," she said, real drawn out and important, and I

wished she wouldn't make such a big deal about it. "I knew this would happen sooner or later, Cynnie."

"It's not a big deal, Kiki."

"That's what you think, girl."

She was curling her eyelashes with one of those awful-looking things women use to curl their eyelashes, and I wondered why it made my eyes water to watch, but not hers to use it.

"What if there's this boy and you're not sure you like him, but you say you'll be his girlfriend. Anyway. Does that make you a wrong kind of person?"

"If you didn't like him, why would you be his girlfriend?"

"Well, let's just say there was something he could do for you. And that's why you wanted to be around him." I felt guilty saying that, because I think there might have been things to like about Snake, other than a car for leaving town. I couldn't think of any right off, but I felt like they were in there somewhere.

Kiki busted up laughing, this really funny sound that squeaked out between her lips like air leaking out of a balloon. "Cynnie, why do you think guys are interested in us? Ever. At all. It's because there's something we can do for them. It's the way of the world, Cynnie. Remember you heard it here first." She bounced up off her chair in front of the makeup mirror and headed for the kitchen.

"So, if guys use us, does that mean if I use a guy back, that's just making it even?"

"That is exactly what I mean. Hey. Cynnie. What happened to all my beer?"

"Beer?"

"Yeah. Beer. I had three cans in here."

"I don't know anything about it, Kiki."

She looked around the corner and raised one eyebrow at me. Damn. Now I'd have to start saving up my lunch money and buying my own.

I didn't see Snake much after school started again, because he was always out at his uncle Ted's junkyard working on the car. In a way it was kind of a relief. I thought he'd be hanging around me all the time. But then I got to feeling sorry for him because it must be lonely out there, with nothing but a bunch of rusty old cars to keep him company. Uncle Ted kept a dog, but it was so mean they only let it out at night.

The day I went to see him was his birthday. I would have felt too creepy not even giving him a present when he was spending all this time fixing up our getaway car.

It was a pretty long way from home, but I rode over on my bike and left it leaning on the office wall of Ted's Auto Parts Recycling. Ted showed me where to find Snake. Good thing he did, too, because there wasn't much to spot him by, just a pair of chunky legs all smeared with grease sticking out from under the car. I was glad when Uncle Ted went back in the office so we could talk.

"So. This is it."

"Yeah. This is it." He didn't come out from under the car, but I heard his voice drift up to me.

"Not bad."

That was just a little lie, and maybe it would make him feel good on his birthday.

It looked pretty crappy. It was a stubby little Nissan, and it was old. I don't know how old, just that it had a lot of rust so you could stick your fingers through in places, and it was bright yellow. I mean bright. It didn't seem like a good car to disappear in. It seemed like people would be staring at us wherever we went.

"Does it run?"

"Not yet. But it will." He still didn't come out.

"I brought you a birthday present."

He grabbed the fender of the car and pulled himself out, and jumped up. He had a big bruise on the side of his face, the whole side, all the way from his forehead down. It looked puffy, and it was more than one color.

"Snake. What happened to your face?"

"Nothing." He was looking at the bag in my hand. The plain brown bag.

I should have wrapped it, I thought, and besides, it was a dumb present, and he'd hate it, and I shouldn't have announced it like that, like it was a big deal, something to look forward to. And then I thought that I'd had lots of days where nothing happened, and it never left a bruise like that on me, and I wondered what happened for real, and why I hadn't brought a better present to make up for it. He reached his hand out and I gave him the bag.

"It's just little," I said.

"Yeah, but you remembered. You came all the way down here."

He stuck his hand into the bag and pulled out the fuzzy dice.

"They're for our new rearview mirror."

"Cool." He stuck his head inside the car and hung them by the little string, and then he came back out and we both admired them from the front. "That looks pretty cool."

He didn't seem disappointed. He had this look on his face. I didn't know quite what it meant. I'd never seen it before. It made me think he was either going to cry or try to kiss me, but then he didn't do either one.

I said, "So, when's the party?"

The look went away. "Never."

"Never? If I just turned fifteen, I'd have a party."

He picked up a wrench and slid back under the car. "I don't like to have anybody over."

"Why not?"

"I just don't, that's all."

He didn't sound like he wanted to talk anymore, so I sat in the passenger seat for a while and closed my eyes and thought about cruising down the road with the window open and all that wind in my face, and Bill on my lap, holding tight to me. Maybe headed for the Grand Canyon.

Then I said goodbye to Snake, and he said goodbye, but he didn't come out from under the car to say it.

I bought one of those big giant beers with my lunch money on the way home, even though I had to ride a mile out of my way to that store where the guy doesn't care how old you are, just so long as you're old enough to pay for it.

I drank it in the alley behind the store, because I knew it

would make it easier to go home. Well, it made it easier to *be* home, but pedaling there on my bike was hard. That street had never seemed so long before.

The more I got into my first year of high school, the more it made me lonely. I don't think I'd ever been lonely before. Or maybe I always had, and I just hadn't known it yet. I didn't have any friends at school, and I didn't really bother to make any. I'd be gone soon anyway, and nobody really acted like they were dying to know me.

I had this feeling like something was missing. It reminded me of that dream where you get to school with no clothes on, but it wasn't that, it was something else. I wanted to talk to Snake but he was kind of quiet, and as soon as school let out, he was gone to Uncle Ted's.

After school I rode around on my bike, to keep from going home. The park sounded like a good idea, until I got there. Then I pedaled across the highway overpass and watched cars shoot by underneath. But only for a minute. Wherever I went, it felt like the wrong place, and I needed to be somewhere else. After a while that made me tired, so I went home, which was worse.

I didn't have anything to drink, and Mom was sitting right by her only bottle and not passed out yet. At first I thought, I'll go without tonight. One night. It'll be good for me. I don't have to drink every night. God, if I drank every night, I'd be starting to be like my mom. Which would be, like, totally disgusting.

But I didn't know what to do. It's like I forgot what I used to do to pass the time. I knew I could read or watch TV, but it sounded boring. It was like my nerves were all bare and everything around me was touching them.

I looked around for money, but my piggy bank was empty. Once I had almost thirty dollars in there. I dug around in my top drawer, thinking maybe I still had a two-dollar bill or some quarters or something. Way in the back I found the three silver dollars from my dad. He gave them to me when I was only three years old. About a week before he died. I quick put them back.

I tried to do something else, or think about something else, but about five minutes later I was on the long walk down to the store with those silver dollars. My stomach felt weird. I was trying not to think at all.

I got a cheap bottle of wine and put it on the counter and then I stood there with those dollars squeezed in my hand. I guess I still had time to change my mind.

"You want that or don't you?" the guy said.

I grabbed the wine and put the dollars on the counter and ran home.

In the morning my stomach felt real heavy and squirrelly just getting up for school. Mom wasn't up, so I poured a little of her gin into my thermos of orange juice, and then I put water in the gin bottle, so it filled up just right. After all, the less gin and the more water she drank, the better. It wouldn't kill her to cut down a little.

Since Bill left, things had only gotten worse with her. It's like she was right in front of my eyes but she didn't exist. It was like living alone. I even wrote to Nanny, telling her that Mom hadn't gotten better at all. She didn't write back for a long time, and when she did she said that grown-up problems were hard, and I should try to be patient. And she said Bill was fine, and he missed me, like I didn't know that already.

I had my own locker at school, and I went back between classes and drank some of the orange juice, and it made the day a lot easier, except it was gone before lunch. It seemed a lot harder to be at school when it was gone, so I left early and rode around on my bike, looking for that right place to be, even though I pretty much knew by then that I'd never find it.

I guess I just figured any day was a good day if it went away and got me one day closer to leaving forever.

One day, while we were waiting to go, I fell asleep in Mr. Werther's art class. I didn't think it was such a big deal, but I guess he did. He told me to wait and talk to him after class. Maybe I fell asleep again, or something close to it, because the bell rang and I remember being really surprised.

I went straight for my locker. I guess I forgot about Mr. Werther. My orange juice was almost gone, and it was only the start of third period. I was just about to toss down the last of it when I saw Mr. Werther standing there watching me. As soon as I saw him I remembered how he told me to stay after class, but it was a little too late by then.

He reached his hand out for the thermos and I gave it to him. Maybe there was a better thing to do at that point, but I couldn't think of it. My brain was working kind of slow.

He smelled it, and then took a little of the orange juice on his finger and tasted it. I expected him to be real mad, but he had a look on his face like he felt sorry for me. I hadn't expected that, and somehow it seemed a lot worse.

The principal said, "This is pretty serious. Do you have anything to say for yourself?"

I said, "No, sir." I wasn't even sure what kind of anything he had in mind. I wasn't sure what people think you're supposed to say when they ask stuff like that.

He sighed. Then he said, "Your mother will have to come down. We'll schedule a special parental meeting to discuss this situation. And there's an automatic three-day suspension. Do you understand?"

"Yes, sir," I said. But I only said that because I knew I was supposed to. I didn't understand. I never understood anybody when they talked. I felt like I was in a country where everybody spoke a different language. And not all of a sudden, either. I'd been feeling that way for as long as I could remember.

"Wait in the outer office. I'll write you a note to take home to her."

I sat there swinging my legs and thinking about when I was littler, and got in trouble, which I almost always did, and how it used to make my stomach tingle. I wondered why my stomach didn't tingle anymore. I knew this wasn't good, but I didn't feel anything about it.

Mrs. Leary, who worked in the office doing attendance, took time off to drive me home.

I kept staring out the window, wondering if I should have

mentioned about my bike still being at school. I got the feeling she was looking at me, but I didn't look back.

"You know," she said, "I've noticed that you miss a lot of afternoon classes. I try to call your mother but she's never home."

"She's home," I said. "She's always home. She just doesn't like to get up and answer the phone." It felt good to run my mom down like that. I'm not sure why.

Mrs. Leary didn't say anything for a long time, but when we pulled into the driveway, she said, "Are you okay at home?"

"Yeah. Fine."

"Anything going on that someone should know about?"

"No. I'm fine."

"We could get you a good counselor."

"I don't need one."

"I think your mother and the principal will decide that. You might not end up with a choice in the matter."

I shrugged. I was thinking, So what's new?

I hoped she'd just drop me off, but she came to the door.

Mom was up, still in her robe, but up. She must've slept late, because I could tell she hadn't had much to drink yet, and I was relieved that she looked okay.

Mrs. Leary said, "Cynthia has a note to explain why she's home in the middle of the day." Then she left us alone.

"So. Where's the note?"

"I think I left it in my locker at school."

"Are you in trouble?"

"Just a little."

"Will you bring the note home tomorrow? Right away?"

"Yeah, I promise."

"Nothing I need to know about sooner?"

"No. No big deal."

She didn't look completely satisfied, but she poured herself a drink and didn't bring it up again. I was kind of relieved and insulted at the same time. It was like she didn't even care enough to find out the truth. It was like she could take anything that pissed her off and just make it evaporate into thin air.

CHAPTER 5

Swimming Upside Down

That night, after it got dark, I slipped out of the house and walked over to Snake's. I figured he'd be home, because he couldn't work on our car in the dark. Maybe we could leave early. Like soon. Like before I had to deal with all the flak. I didn't know if the car was ready, but I knew it ran. I hadn't actually seen it run, but I'd been told. I was so ready to disappear, I felt like I was about to explode. And I wanted to see Bill so bad. I felt like another ten minutes would be too long to wait.

Snake's father answered the door. He was a big man with hair all bushy on the sides and missing completely on top. He had a plastic bag full of ice on his eye, and before I even said anything I could tell he was in a bad mood.

"Is Snake home?"

"No."

"Oh. Do you know where he is?"

"No."

"Oh. Maybe when he gets back—"

"He won't, if he's smart."

"Oh. Okay. Bye."

I walked as fast as I could back to the street, but the door was still open, and I thought I could feel him watching me. It felt like something cold all down my back. I tried not to run.

I had no idea Snake's dad was so scary. I guess he didn't want me to know.

I decided I'd a million times rather live with my mom than Snake's dad. I decided Snake's got it worse than me.

Halfway home I saw Snake coming right down the sidewalk at me. He had a big towel that he was holding up to his mouth and a lot of blood on his shirt. So I felt partly scared about what happened to him and partly glad to see him.

I said, "Snake. What happened?"

He said, "You want to get out of this town, you better pack. Your ride's leaving."

I really, really wished he could have said something friendlier to me. I needed someone to be friendly. And usually Snake was. See? This is why you should never think you've got something in somebody.

I said we should sleep first. I said, "I could slip you into my house, and we'll leave in the morning, when it's light." When everything would seem friendlier, I was thinking. But I didn't want to say that.

Snake said, "When we're out of this town, then I'll sleep."

He went to get the car, and I went to my room to pack. It was hard to know what to take. First I wanted to take everything, like it was all me, then I got frustrated and decided nothing meant anything, anyway. Only Bill was important. I could hear Snake doing little beeps on the horn out back. I stuffed my suitcases with clothes and left everything else except my diary. The more of my old life I left behind, the better.

Mom was passed out on the couch. I snapped my fingers, but she didn't open her eyes. So I said goodbye to her. That way she could never say I left without even saying goodbye. It wasn't my fault if she was too drunk to notice. It wasn't my fault if she got to disappear first.

We were twenty miles out of town before I got Snake to show me what was under the towel. He had a big split in his lower lip, and it was all puffed up and still bleeding. I said I thought maybe he'd need stitches for that, but he shook his head. I think it's because stitches would have been expensive, but I'm not sure. He didn't much want to talk, and I didn't blame him.

After an hour or two we found a place to pull off onto a dirt road. Not much traffic. He put the seat back and closed his eyes. I couldn't figure out if he was asleep or not.

I guess that was a moment I'd been worried about. Like Snake might suddenly announce it was time to be his girlfriend for real. But he was upset, and his mouth must've hurt. I think he wanted to be left alone. In fact, he was acting like he *was* alone, like I wasn't there at all.

I could hear crickets and some yapping noises that might have been dogs or coyotes. And a car now and then on the highway. I closed my eyes and it all sounded so loud to me, and I wondered if this was how you felt if you were blind and everything else got much clearer.

I could see my mom's face behind my eyelids, and it was almost hard to believe I didn't live there with her anymore. How could so much have changed so fast? It was such a weird feeling.

I said, "Now I'm thinking my mom wasn't so bad." I said it out loud to Snake, even though I didn't know if he was listening. He didn't say anything, and he didn't open his eyes, but I kept talking. "At least when she got mad she slapped instead of punching. Nothing on me ever got bruised up or bloody."

I was actually starting to wish I was home. At least at home you always know what's going to happen. You know it's going to be bad, but at least you know.

I looked over at Snake and I saw he was crying a little. It made me feel terrible. I thought at least Snake knew what he was doing. Even if I didn't.

"Snake," I said. "Please don't cry."

He said something I couldn't understand. His lip had been swelling up, and now you couldn't even tell what he was saying. But from the way he said it, I had a feeling he was trying to say he wasn't crying. He turned his face partway away so I couldn't see.

"Everybody cries," I said, and then he started crying a lot

harder, so it was way too late to pretend. He just sort of came apart when I said that.

I wasn't sure what to do. I did the only thing I could think of. I moved the towel away and I kissed him. Just kind of quick. Just for a second.

He made the weirdest noise. It was like a giant grunt, like a big, dangerous animal roaring out loud. It scared me. I thought, you're not supposed to make a sound like that when somebody kisses you. Are you? His hand flew up to his lip and I realized I'd hurt him.

"Oh, Snake. I'm sorry. Did I make it bleed again?"

I reached up to try to turn on the inside light of the car but he was trying to say something to me, something I couldn't make out. It was like other people trying to understand Bill. Finally I got what he was saying.

"Doesn't work."

I guess I should have figured in an old car like this one, the light wouldn't work. I never did find out if I made his lip bleed again.

"I'm sorry, Snake."

"It's okay," he said, or something like that. He mumbled something that made it sound like it was okay.

I put my head down on his shoulder and I put my arms around him, like I do with Bill when he's upset. We tried to go to sleep. I was pretty scared for sleeping, though. I felt like I might never sleep again.

Then I thought about Bill, and how soon I'd see him, and that put me in a much better mood.

❖ ❖ ❖

Snake dropped me two blocks from Nanny and Grampop's house. We agreed to meet at the gas station three blocks over when I was done, which probably wouldn't be until nearly morning.

I felt bad that Snake had to sleep in the car again, but I couldn't think of any way around that. It was about dinnertime.

I said, "I'll sneak you something if I possibly can."

"Thank you," he said. "That would be nice." Then he said, "We should think where we're going. We should have a plan."

I didn't really like the idea of a plan. I just wanted to disappear. I didn't even want to know to where. Just like those kids in Zack's story—when they climbed up in those trees, they didn't have a plan.

"Maybe we'll talk about that later," I said.

My knees felt kind of gooey and shaky while I walked up their driveway. Mom must have called them by now. Any fool could figure I'd show up wherever Bill was, first thing. Didn't take a high school graduate to figure that out.

I'd never been a very good liar—people seemed to look right through me like I was a fishbowl or something. But I'd better get good, and fast. Bill's future was at stake. Oh yeah, and mine, too.

Nanny came to the door. Her hair wasn't perfect. It threw me off completely. I forgot what I'd planned to say first.

"Cynthia. Thank God. Your mother's been worried sick about you."

"I'm surprised she noticed I was gone." I meant to say something nicer and more cooperative, but that's what came out. It felt like I couldn't pass up a chance to run her down. It was like letting something out that had to get out. Something that was clawing me to death from the inside.

"Now, now. Let's not talk like that. Come in, dear. How did you get here? Do you want us to drive you home?"

"First I want to see Bill." As soon as I said his name, I heard him in the next room, saying, "Thynnie. Thynnie." All of a sudden my whole life felt sad, everybody's whole life. The whole world got sadder than it had been a minute ago, and I started to cry, even though I tried real hard to keep it in. "Please just let me see Bill."

She didn't answer, so I walked past her and followed his voice. He was in a playpen in the living room, bouncing up and down because he could hear me but he couldn't get to me.

I picked him up. I felt real bad because I couldn't tell him it wasn't my idea, his going away. I guess that was the part I'd always felt worst about, that I couldn't tell him how hard I'd fought. It was such an awful thought that I hadn't really had it until just that moment.

He kept saying, "Thynnie. Thynnie." It was like a song. Something that made me feel really good inside. It's funny how easy it is to lose track of why anything means anything, and then all of a sudden something reminds you. I hugged him, and we rocked back and forth. He was heavier than I re-membered, but I didn't put him down.

Nanny was standing behind me. I didn't know how long

she'd been there. She said, "We just finished dinner, but I'll make you up a plate. Then you'll get a good night's sleep, and Grampop will drive you home in the morning."

I slipped a plastic bag out of her kitchen drawer and stuck it in my pocket. She gave me a plate of chicken and French fries and coleslaw. I asked to take it upstairs to Bill's room. I said I was tired and upset and needed privacy, which was not entirely lying.

I ate the coleslaw, because it would have made everything else soggy, and I put the chicken and French fries in the bag, and then after a few minutes I went downstairs and asked for seconds.

Nanny came into our room right before we put the lights out. I still hadn't seen Grampop, and I was a little worried about that, because maybe he was too mad to talk to me.

Nanny said, "Why, Cynthia? What was the point of worrying us like that?"

"I have a right to see Bill."

"Why didn't you ask?"

"Oh, sure. Like she would have let me."

"You still have to do things the right way."

I think my whole life changed, just in that second. Because I'd been *trying* to do things the right way, my whole life. The way everybody told me life is supposed to work. And when Nanny said that, it got so clear that it was all a crock. Their way doesn't get you anywhere. I felt like I was swimming in a pool and I was pushing to get to the top and then just when I expected to break the surface and breathe air I hit my head on the bottom. You know how that feels? Like you were so sure it was up but all of a sudden you find out it was down, and you can't imagine how you could've been so wrong. How everything could be so the opposite of what you thought.

I knew the next words out of my mouth would be a lie. Because I was done trying to talk to Nanny. I was done telling the truth.

"Well, I'm sorry I worried everybody, Nanny. I'll go home in the morning." She didn't seem to know that none of that was true. Then, before she got out the door, I said, "She hasn't changed at all."

"Give it time, dear."

"I tried that. It's just getting worse. Her new boyfriend is a total loser, and now that Bill's gone she does even less around the house. You really didn't help at all. You said you'd talk to her and you didn't help."

I probably shouldn't have said all that. I'd broken my own promise, not to even try with her anymore. Besides, what did it matter? I was never going to see any of them again. I wanted to see if Nanny had that special hurt look on, but the light was off, and the light from the hallway just lit her up from behind, like a ghost or an angel.

She said, "We'll talk in the morning, dear." Her voice sounded funny and stiff.

No, we won't, I thought. In the morning it'll be a whole new world. I lay awake in bed whistling the theme from *Star Trek*, and Bill sang it back to me. Before morning we were boldly going . . . I don't know. Somewhere. Anywhere would be better.

I fell asleep without meaning to. When I woke up, the house was quiet. It was about eleven-thirty. I got Bill dressed and threw two drawers full of his clothes in a bag. The floor had one squeaky board, and I had to be careful not to step on it.

I slipped downstairs and took a couple of swigs of Grampop's Scotch. I thought a little would take the edge off how bad I felt, but as soon as I drank a little I felt like I needed to drink more. I tried not to think about that. I tried to just think about getting Bill and getting out.

I looked around to make sure the coast was clear. Good thing I did. I ran smack into Grampop, sitting at the kitchen table eating a piece of leftover cake.

"Couldn't sleep?" he said.

"Guess not."

I sat down at the table with him. He wouldn't look at me. Grown-ups are funny when they're mad. Funny strange, I mean. They never admit it straight out, but any fool can see.

"Your mother has a hard enough time without you pulling stunts."

I wanted to say, *She* makes her life hard, not me. I wanted to say, Seeing my little brother who got stolen from me is not a stunt. But I didn't. Because it didn't matter anymore. I didn't have to make my family understand me now. It was easier to just go away, where I didn't have to watch them disapprove.

We didn't talk for a while, and then Grampop got up and went to bed. He didn't even say good night. He didn't even rinse his dish, so I rinsed it for him. I looked out the window until I was sure he'd gone to bed. And I wondered how things had gotten so complicated. But as far as I could remember, they always had been. I couldn't remember when life had ever been any easier than this.

It was after midnight when Bill and I got back to the car. I woke Snake up and gave him the chicken and French fries. That made him happy. Bill looked at Snake and Snake looked at Bill and I knew we didn't have any love-at-first-sight situation on our hands. I think they made each other nervous more than anything else.

When Snake was done eating, I had him drive by the house. I couldn't carry everything, so I'd left a bunch of things on the lawn. A suitcase with Bill's stuff, clothes and toys and things, all except his elephant, which he had tight under his arm. And a bag with some cheese and a loaf of bread and a bag of nacho chips and some sodas that I'd borrowed from the fridge. And a big bottle of Grampop's Scotch that I thought would be nice to have on the road. We got all this stuff into the backseat, and then we headed for Arizona.

I rolled my window down and took a blast of cool night air in the face, and I felt like I could breathe for the first time. For the first time ever I'd dreamed about something and now here it was, just the way I wanted it. A whole new world. I hugged Bill tighter on my lap.

I opened the bottle of Scotch and took a few swallows. I think I might've promised myself I wouldn't after I got Bill back. But this was different. When I promised that I thought we'd be at home, all nice and safe.

Snake gave me a dirty look.

"What's your problem?" I said, and Bill got nervous right away, sensing a fight.

"We're both underage, and I don't have a license. Just what I need is one more thing to get arrested for."

I said, "Yeah, well, if they stop us they can only arrest us once. Stop worrying."

"Dynamite logic," he said, and I realized we were fighting, just like a real boyfriend and girlfriend. That made my stomach uneasy, so I sipped a little more Scotch, and it settled down some.

"Let's go to the Grand Canyon," I said. Snake didn't answer one way or another.

I felt cheated, because all of a sudden he was in a rotten mood all the time. I thought he'd be good company, but it wasn't like I'd pictured it at all.

Boy, if I thought that was a fight, I had no idea. Come nightfall we were all the way to Williams, Arizona. We found a place to park but it was cold, and we were both tired. We had enough money for one more tank of gas. Then we had a problem to solve.

He said, "How are we supposed to be alone, anyway?"

I wasn't sure what to say. I didn't want to be alone with him yet, but that might not have been the best answer. "Lay off Bill. I told you it was no deal without him."

"It's like we're an old married couple already. No privacy. The kid comes first."

"You knew it was going to be this way, Snake, so lay off. You're being a jerk."

68

"Oh, *I'm* being a jerk. Right. It's always my fault."

"Look," I said. "Forget the Grand Canyon. You need to get some sleep, and we need to get where we're going."

"Where are we going?"

"I don't know. Somewhere. Farther away than this. I'll drive all night. You'll feel better in the morning."

"You? You can't drive."

"Why can't I?"

"It takes practice."

"Get real. You put it in drive, and you steer so you stay in the same lane. It's freeway all the way through."

"What if we get pulled over?"

"Then we're dead one way or another. Neither one of us has a license."

We argued around about it until Bill started to cry, and then Snake gave up.

"Fine," he said. "Only be careful."

CHAPTER 6

Trouble

I tried to put Bill in the backseat, but he was feeling extra clingy. So I let him sit on my lap and I put the seat belt around both of us. It took me a minute to get used to the gas pedal, how hard to press, but once I got out on the freeway it seemed easy.

Snake put his seat back and closed his eyes, and then the whole world got quiet. I liked the dark road. I liked Bill on my lap. I was whispering to him the whole time, telling him how good everything was going to be. How we'd live in a new place where no one would tell us what to do. The more I talked, the more he got nervous. If it hadn't been for Bill, I wouldn't have known I was lying. Underneath all my happy talk it seemed so scary, headed out into the night, headed for a new place, when we didn't even know where the new place was. How would we know when we got there?

I opened the Scotch again and took a few slugs. I could feel it burn down into my belly, right where I needed it. The nice thing about a drink is that it can always find the place that needs warming up. After a while I felt real mellow and good. I was thinking that a bottle is the one thing that never lets you down. You think you know what it'll do for you, and you're always right. Not like people at all. Not like any other part of life. I could hear Snake snoring a little, and Bill fell asleep with his head halfway under my arm. That made it harder to steer but I didn't want to disturb him.

I wished somebody would wake up and talk to me. I felt kind of alone. I kept thinking that at home, I had my mom to take care of things. Which is a joke, because she never did, only it seemed like it had helped me some, knowing she was there. Who was going to take care of everything now? I took a few more sips.

I really didn't drink that much, though. I mean, I was driving. For the first time ever.

I rolled down the window and the night came in and hit me in the face. I figured it would keep me awake, at least. I guess that's when I got the feeling I had about speed. I guess until I felt that air rush in, I didn't realize I was going fast. But the way it blew into my face made me think about riding on Zack's motorcycle. I remembered the way he hit the gas, and it made the wind blow around in my shirt. Then I thought

71

about that night on the porch when I asked what made him feel whole for a second. Driving his bike too fast. That was the first thing he said, without even thinking. I wanted real bad to feel whole, so I decided to try it his way.

I put the gas pedal all the way down. It took a minute for that poor tired old car to get it together, but then we were going really good. The night wind in my face was making me squint and pushing tears out of my eyes.

I got this great rush where I felt like, Yeah. This is what we do. We do crazy shit, because we're broken. That's who we are. That's what we do.

Then I saw flashing red lights come on in my rearview mirror. And I knew I was dead.

I stomped on the gas even harder. I didn't know what else to do. I guess I thought I could still get away. I don't know what I thought. It was too much trouble to stop and face, so I just stomped on the gas.

I heard a siren, and the lights kept up with me, and then I saw the road was curving, but by the time I saw guardrail coming right at me, it was too late.

I tried to turn, but I think I pulled the wheel too hard. The car seemed to spin like it was alive on its own. No matter what I did it wouldn't stop spinning.

We spun all the way across the freeway, three lanes, and I could hear Snake yelling.

There was a guardrail on the other side, too, and we were headed right for it. I tried stomping on the brake, but the car was spinning all on its own and I think that made it worse. So

I just closed my eyes and braced for it. There was nothing else I could do.

It just all happened so fast.

When I woke up I was in the hospital. It was late, and it was dark, and nobody was there but me. There wasn't even anybody in the other bed. It was sort of spooky.

Then I guess I went back to sleep again, because when I woke up, it was light. There was a nurse standing over my bed. She was black, and really pretty, with that great kind of hair that's all little tiny braids. I wished my hair would do that.

"You're awake," she said.

"I guess."

My left leg felt really heavy, like I almost couldn't feel it, but I knew it was there because it hurt. And the left side of my head hurt, too.

"You might be about to wish you never woke up," she said.

"Why? What do you mean?" I couldn't get my brain to work right. It wasn't clear.

"I mean, you are in quite a mess of trouble, girl. A great big old mess. I wouldn't want to trade places with you, that's what I'm saying. There were a couple of highway patrol guys in here waiting for you to wake up. I guess they're waiting to finish their report. They finally gave up. But they'll be back. Don't you worry."

Then she did something to the plastic bag that was hanging up beside the bed, dripping something down through a tube and into the back of my hand.

73

All of a sudden I thought about Bill. "What about Bill?" I said. "Is Bill okay?"

"Which one is Bill? The little guy or the big guy?"

"The little one."

"He's in stable condition, I think. I think he's listed as stable. Got a mess of broken ribs. One of them punctured his lung. But he'll be okay. By and by."

"Can I see him? I really need to see him."

"Oh, I doubt that," she said. "I wouldn't count on that."

"But I need to see him."

"He's fine," she said. "You just worry about your own self. You need all the worry you got. Good luck." Then she left, just like that. I couldn't tell if she really, actually felt sorry for me or not.

I tried to lift my left hand to feel the side of my head. See if I could tell why it hurt so much. But it didn't lift, and I was really sorry I tried, right away. That arm was all bruised up. I couldn't really use it for anything. I used my right instead. I had a little bandage on the left side of my head, and I couldn't tell for sure but I think it had stitches under it. The rest of that side of my face felt too big, and it hurt to touch it.

There was a button on the bed with me, with a cord, and it said it was for calling the nurse. I pressed it so she would come back. And then I waited. But I didn't get her. I got a skinny white nurse with a tight face who didn't look nearly as nice.

"Yes, darling?" she said, but she didn't sound like she thought I was all that darling.

"I need to see my brother, Bill," I said. "It's really important." I couldn't tell her how much or why. I couldn't even tell myself yet. If Bill was hurt bad and it was all my fault . . .

"That's out of the question, dear. You're to stay in bed and be still, and so is he."

"Could you go see him for me and tell me for sure he's okay?"

She sighed. "Honey, I've got a lot of patients to look after. He's in stable condition. If his condition changes, I promise I'll let you know."

Then she bustled out before I could argue.

I lay awake for a long time and thought about the day before I left home. I remembered how I wanted to get away real fast, because I was in trouble. I was ready to do anything not to have to face all that.

But now I couldn't even think how much trouble I was in. I couldn't even get my brain to stretch that far. I would have done anything to be back at home, showing my mom that note from the principal, listening to her yell at me for stealing her gin. That wasn't even hardly trouble. I'd've killed for that kind of trouble now.

A little later on the nice nurse stuck her head back through my door. "Seen those highway patrol guys yet?"

"Not yet."

She made a sound, the kind of sound you make when you just scraped out of a bad situation. Kind of a big long "phew" sound. Only I wasn't out of this one yet. Not by a long shot.

"Will you do something for me?" I asked. "It's really important." As soon as I said how important it was, I started to cry.

That's when I could tell, by her face, that she really did feel bad for me.

"Could you go check on my brother Bill and tell me for a fact that he's okay?"

She sighed, just like the other nurse. "I guess," she said. "I guess, when I get a second."

I waited for what felt like hours, and I never really got to crying all the way—the kind of crying that washes it out of you and makes you feel better—but I couldn't exactly stop, either.

Then she stuck her head back in. "He's doing okay," she said. "His poor little ribs are all taped up. But he's awake and all. He's saying something. I can't tell what it is, though."

"Thynnie," I said.

She tilted her head and looked at me funny. "Yeah. How'd you know that?"

"It's the only word Bill knows how to say."

"What does it mean?"

"It means me."

After she left I thought about how bad I wanted something to drink. I had those needles in my stomach, and this feeling like I was walking into a dark room that had a monster in it but I didn't know where he was. I knew I couldn't stand to feel this way for long. But I couldn't figure out how to get to anything, or how to get anything to me. What a time to get stuck with just myself.

That night, while I was sleeping, I felt a hand touching my arm. My good arm. I thought it was the nurse. I didn't understand why she had to wake me up. Every time I woke up I just felt hurt and scared. I just wanted to stay asleep. But then the hand was shaking me.

I opened my eyes. At first it was too dark to see much. But then my eyes got used to the dark and I saw it was Snake.

"Snake," I said. "Are you okay?"

"Yeah," he said. "But I'm leaving."

"What do you mean, leaving? Where are you going? Did you get hurt bad?"

"Not so bad," he said. "It was a lot worse on your side of the car."

"Do me a favor?" I said. "Can you go by Bill's room and tell him I never meant for him to get hurt?"

He didn't say anything for a long time. I didn't think it was such a big deal, what I asked. Especially since he wasn't hurt that bad.

"Did you hear what I said, Cynnie? I'm leaving. This is it. The end of the line. The last we see each other."

"Where are you going?"

"I don't know. But I'm not going home. They called my dad to come get me. So I have to get away before he gets here. Because I'm not going back with my dad."

"But . . . what'll you do?"

"I don't know. Something. I'll think of something."

I guess it was a weird question, asking him what he was going to do. Because we'd already run away. What were the two of us going to do when we took off from home? Why should this be any harder? I guess it had dawned on me more, since all this happened, how much bad stuff can happen out there in the world. I guess it didn't seem like such a small thing anymore, taking off with no money and no plan, not even knowing what you're going to do to be okay.

"So will you tell Bill that for me before you go?"

He made a sound that was almost like laughing. But it wasn't a happy laugh. I could tell nothing was funny for real. "Nice to know you're gonna miss me so much," he said. He got up and walked halfway to the door. Then he stopped, but he didn't even turn around to look at me. He just talked like he was talking to the door. "I really liked you," he said.

I said the only thing I could think to say. "Why?" I said it like it was a great big mystery. It was. I really couldn't imagine.

"I guess I thought we sort of . . . you know . . . understood each other. Or something. Like not everybody knows what it's like to be us. But we know."

Nobody said anything for a long time. I wondered if I was supposed to say something. Maybe I was supposed to say I liked him, too.

"Did you ever even like me?" he asked.

I didn't know what to say. I remembered Kiki telling me that guys only like us because there's something we can do for them. I was counting on her to be right. I was counting on it not really mattering much if I felt anything for Snake or not.

I figured he wouldn't care about that. But maybe Kiki was wrong.

I guess I wasn't answering fast enough.

"Right," he said. "Got it."

He walked out, and the door came swishing back with a big sound of air. It was like somebody had shut the door on my life. It was like there was no more sky, and all the air you used to be able to breathe got sucked away.

It was like I didn't have one single thing left.

In the morning the highway patrol guys came into my room. One of them had a clipboard. They both had guns and very neat uniforms, and I could see to look at them why the nurse made that "phew" sound. They were two scary guys.

The first thing they asked me is whose idea was it for me to be driving the car.

"Mine," I said.

"The boy didn't talk you into it?"

"No."

"You sure?"

"Positive. I had to talk him into letting me drive."

We went around and around about this for a long time. I got the feeling they wanted it to be mostly Snake's fault. Maybe because he was a boy, or because he was older. Maybe it was just because he was gone.

I thought about it, too, for a second. He's gone, anyway, and they can't do anything to him. I could try to put it off on him. But I couldn't. I just couldn't. Snake had never done anything bad to me. Not one thing I could think of, and I really tried. I wanted to think of one time he stabbed me in the back, so I could blame all this on him. But there was nothing.

"No," I said. "I drove because I wanted to."

I wasn't even still trying to save myself. I just sort of held my nose and sank all the way down into trouble.

The day I left the hospital I had to sit up in a wheelchair so the nurse could wheel me down to the lobby. It was the middle of the morning, and I knew my mom was around here somewhere or they wouldn't be checking me out. But I hadn't actually seen her. It was like this big black cloud of doom sitting on my head. It was like knowing you were going to die in about three minutes. It seemed weird that she hadn't even tried to come sooner. Just when she absolutely had to, to give me a ride. It sort of sucked, but then I was relieved to put off seeing her. So I didn't know how to feel about that.

Getting into the wheelchair wasn't easy. I had a big, heavy cast on my leg, and the nurse had to help me hold it, and it really hurt to move. My left arm still couldn't do much, so it was hard to lower myself into the chair without bumping around a lot. All through this awful stuff, I was wanting to ask her something, but I was afraid what she would say.

Just as she was wheeling me into the hallway, I spit it out. "Can we go by Bill's room, real quick? Just so I can see him?"

"Honey, he's gone."

My stomach got all cold. I felt like somebody had hit me in the gut with a piece of lumber. My brain was tingling. "What do you mean, gone?"

"Your grandma and grampa came and picked him up."

I breathed again for the first time in what felt like a long time. I couldn't even say out loud what I'd been thinking for a second there. I thought she meant he was gone, like . . . I couldn't even bring myself to think it. All the way down, my legs and my stomach were all shivery from what I thought for just that second.

She wheeled me right through the lobby and out the door, like she expected my mom to come driving up any second. But I still hadn't seen her. It was cloudy outside, but kind of heavy wet and warm. The clouds were dark, and I looked up at them, and they looked like I felt.

"They never even came in and talked to me."

"Who?"

"Nanny and Grampop."

"Oh."

I knew why, too. I didn't even have to ask. They were so mad at me, they didn't even want to see me. They couldn't even look at me. It was that bad. And I never even got to tell Bill I was sorry. For the second time, he was gone, and I didn't even get to say goodbye.

"Why does life get so awful sometimes?" I asked her.

She thought that over a minute, like she had to be sure. "Sometimes, I don't know," she said. "Sometimes it seems like it just is. No matter what you do. But other times it's because you're doing what you shouldn't be doing and not doing what you should."

"Oh," I said.

Then I was sorry I even asked.

I shouldn't have worried about that moment when my mom came to get me. Because she didn't. Kiki did. First I thought that was a good break. But I was wrong. About an hour into the drive she dropped a major artillery shell.

"Don't take this personally or anything," she said. "But I'm out."

I didn't know out of what. And I didn't want to ask, because it sounded serious.

"You know I don't do the whole *Mom* thing, Cynnie. You know that." She waited, like I might have something to say. Wrong. "You have no idea how I caught hell over this. She figures it's partly my fault, because you come over to talk. And sometimes I give you advice, yeah. But I didn't tell you to do *this* fool thing."

That just sat in the air for a while. Too long.

"So what are you saying, Kiki? That I can't come over anymore?"

"I'm not getting involved with this family again. I won't do it. We're talking survival here. I'd help you if I could. I'm sorry. But this is about my own survival."

"So I'm just never going to see you?"

"When you're older and you don't live with her. When you're on your own, fine."

Great. A mere five years away. In other words, we'd see each other in my next lifetime.

It was a quiet drive after that.

A few miles later she said, "I'm sorry, Cynnie. I really am."

I said, "Whatever."

It's not like I didn't know that's how things turn out. It's not like I wasn't used to it.

CHAPTER 7

My Scratchy New World

It was a whole new world, all right. I should be careful what I wish for. And, also, I was wrong about the part where nobody would tell me what to do.

Mom drove me to my first court-ordered AA meeting.

"Why don't you come in?" I said. "You might get something out of this, too." I guess it sounded snotty. Maybe it was, but I really didn't mean it that way. I was scared, and wanting company.

She got pissed. She'd been on a real short fuse ever since she had to go to Arizona for court and all.

"Don't you turn this around on me, young lady. This is not about what *I* did."

"Yeah, yeah. All right."

"I'll be back at nine-thirty."

Damn. No way to duck out early. I was too far from home to walk, at least in my condition.

I limped inside. There were people coming in, and more inside milling around. One of them held the door for me, because of my crutches and all. Everybody kept trying to catch my eye and smile at me. The last thing I wanted was to look in anybody's eyes.

I headed for the table with coffee and cookies. I wanted to get myself a cup of coffee, but I felt like everybody was watching me, and everybody would think I was too young. So I ate nine cookies. I kept wishing the meeting would start so we would all have someplace to look.

The walls were covered with cardboard signs, and they said things like "One day at a time" and "Easy does it." Whatever that means.

This woman came up to me and offered her hand to shake. I didn't want to take it. I already knew I didn't like her.

"I'm Pat," she said.

"Okay."

"Welcome."

I guess I kind of snorted. I didn't want to be welcome because I didn't want to be here at all. I wanted to crawl under the table and never come out. I looked at the door, and I think I would have run, except I had a broken leg, and besides, I knew my mom was going to ask to see my court card, to make sure I got it signed.

Pat said, "You remind me a lot of me."

I didn't take that as a compliment. Because she was old. About fifty. And real heavy. I mean, there was a whole lot of her. I ate two more cookies.

She said, "When I was your age, I mean. I was only fourteen when I came to my first meeting."

I couldn't think of anything to say. In my head I kept saying, Leave me alone. Leave me alone. I didn't think it would be like this. I thought I could sit in the back and think about something else.

"Isn't that about how old you are?"

"Next month."

"I hope you do better than I did. I didn't believe I was an alcoholic, so I went out and stayed drunk for another eleven years. Is this your first meeting?"

"Yeah. I don't belong here." There was no point trying to really explain to anybody what a total misunderstanding this all was. I mean, I guess I could see how the judge got it wrong. Because I did have some alcohol in me at the time of the accident. But nobody knew about driving fast to try not to feel broken, and I wasn't about to explain it. It was between me and one other person, and that's the way it would stay.

"Oh. Okay. I guess that's what I thought, too. I guess somewhere, sometime, somebody must wander into these rooms who doesn't belong here. But not often."

"I'm only here 'cause I got ordered here by a judge."

"See, you remind me more of me all the time. I was in trouble when I first came, too."

Stop talking to me, stop talking to me. It was a chant that I kept to myself. It didn't work.

"Maybe we can talk after the meeting."

"Nah, my mom's picking me up. Right after."

"Tomorrow morning, maybe. We could have breakfast and talk about the twelve steps."

"Saturday mornings I have to see my probation officer."

"I see. Pretty complicated life for a kid not even fourteen."

"Just the way things go sometimes."

A man sitting at the head of the table spoke up real loud. He said, "My name is Tom, and I'm an alcoholic." Everybody said, "Hi, Tom." I thought, Oh, brother. But at least it meant the meeting was starting. And Pat would go sit down.

The leader gave out some little plastic medallions to people who had thirty days, or six months, or a year without drinking, and some others in between. They called them chips. He also wanted to give a welcome chip to anybody who was coming to their first meeting. I wouldn't catch anybody's eye or say a word, and after a while the meeting went on, and I breathed again. This was not the way I thought it would be. I thought it would be like school. Sit in the back, don't raise your hand, and it's like you're not there at all.

Pat sat right next to me, and I couldn't think of any way to fix that. I hated it when people took an interest in me. It made me really nervous. She was watching me out of the corner of her eye. I tried to pretend I was listening to the leader, but he was so boring. All he was saying was stuff that reminded me of Mom. Getting drunk earlier and earlier at night, and throwing up in the morning. I guess that's the first time it hit me that my mom really was an alcoholic. I could tell because all their stories sounded just like her. And if she was, then I definitely wasn't. I wasn't that bad.

Then I looked up to the door and saw Zack come in. I couldn't swallow, and I could hear my own heart beating. I could see Pat watching me but I'm not sure if I cared anymore.

He was so much better-looking than I remembered. He sat down on the other side of the room. His hair had grown out, and it looked real nice, and his eyes scanned up and down the tables until he saw me. He looked a little bit surprised. Then he smiled, real wide and nice, like he did that day out by the reservoir, and he winked at me.

It was a way only Bill had ever made me feel: like there's something on this old, dried-up planet that's really worth the price of admission, that almost makes up for everything else.

Maybe I'd come to a meeting every day, instead of three times a week. My probation officer would like that.

I was thinking next time I'd bring a pencil and some paper. I thought if I could stare at the side of his face like this all during a meeting, I could draw his picture. Usually I hated whatever pictures I drew, but somehow I thought I'd like this one, because it would be Zack.

Then all of a sudden somebody called on me and asked if I'd like to say anything. I could feel Zack's eyes on me, and my face felt frozen, and I knew I couldn't talk. My heart got loud again.

Something funny happened inside. I thought about Snake.

I thought about how he spent all that time fixing up the car and I wrecked it, and how I got him in trouble, and I wondered where he was and if he was okay. Mostly I thought about the way I felt when I looked at Zack, and I knew I was supposed to feel that way with Snake, and it wasn't fair to him that I never did. I had this strange idea that someday I'd sit in a run-down room like this one, sharing stories about all the people I'd hurt with my drinking, and I'd mention Snake and say I'd apologize to him, except he was gone.

While I was thinking this, everybody was staring at me. But they all looked nice, and smiled in a nice way. Very patient while I made an idiot of myself.

I thought, This is not like the real world, where people make fun of you at a time like this. I thought, This place is weird.

"My name is Cynnie," I said. That's how everybody else started.

Everybody said, "Hi, Cynnie." All at once. It made me jump.

They probably wanted me to say I was an alcoholic. Good luck on that. The judge said I had to come. He didn't say I had to lie. "Uh. Maybe I'll talk next time."

Everybody smiled and nodded, like I'd said something brilliant, and then someone said, "Welcome, Cynnie," and then everybody said it. My face felt burning hot. Then somebody else got picked to talk.

I never heard a word of what anybody said. Oh, a word here or there, stuff about driving drunk and going to jail, but it never seemed to add up to anything. I kept staring at the side of Zack's face. I was so happy to see him, but it felt funny, too.

I kept thinking he didn't belong here. That I didn't want him to be here. That somehow by being here he was walking out on something we used to share.

Then I decided it might be a small price to pay for finding him again. I mean, I thought he'd disappeared, that I'd lost him forever. And now, here we both were.

After the meeting my mom was late, as always. Pat walked me out to the street, and I kept wishing my mom would hurry up and come, so I could get away. Pat said that if I felt I was ready for a sponsor, she'd be happy to help. I wasn't sure what that meant.

After a while I saw Zack come down the steps behind us. I kept looking over my shoulder until I saw him.

"Excuse me," I said to Pat, and walked away before she could say anything back.

My throat got kind of tight as I walked up to him, and I got scared that maybe when I opened my mouth, I wouldn't be able to squeeze anything out.

I had no idea what to say, so I said, "Hey, Zack. Can I bum a cigarette?"

He frowned, and then I got even more scared, because that had been the very safest thing I could think of to say, and from the look on his face it was the worst thing possible.

"Oh. Funny you should mention that," he said. "I owe you an amends for something."

I had no idea what he meant. Well, no, that's not true. I sort of knew what the word meant. Regretting something and trying to make it right. But most people didn't say it like that. Just that they were sorry. He motioned to the concrete stairs of the meeting place, and we sat down. I was wanting that cigarette more than ever, and I couldn't figure out why he wouldn't give me one.

"I feel pretty damn guilty," he said. "Seeing you at an AA meeting when I'm probably the one who gave you your first beer."

I wanted to say a hundred different things at once. I wanted to say it was all a big mistake, my having to come here. That the trouble I got into really wasn't about drinking. Not so much as people thought. It was about wanting to drive too fast to see how it felt. To be more like him. And then everybody got the wrong idea. I wanted to say that I liked what he opened up for me when he gave me cigarettes and beer. That I hated to hear him talk about that now like it wasn't a good thing. It all got tangled up on itself, though. There was just too much of it. I couldn't figure out what to say first, or how to say any of it so it would make sense.

Instead I just said, "It was really more like my second or third."

"It was still wrong of me. You're thirteen years old."

"Nearly fourteen."

"You weren't nearly fourteen at the time."

"Well. That's true."

Then the guy who had to clean up from the meeting came out and locked the door, and walked by us down the stairs. He

91

stopped for a minute to say good night to Zack and to tell me to keep coming back, and I wished he would go away so I could be alone with Zack to talk.

I had this awful thought that maybe he wasn't broken anymore. Maybe now that was only me.

When the guy finally left I said, "Do you still drive your motorcycle too fast?"

"Oh, I'm trying to slow down," he said. "I'm getting a little better."

I was thinking fast was better, but before I could say anything, my mom drove up.

Zack walked up to our car, and my mom rolled the window down. It looked like she was trying to talk or swallow or both, and not doing too good with either.

"Hello, Rita."

Nothing. Just her big eyes. Then she said, "How long have you been coming here?"

"Got sixty days last Friday."

"Good. That's good." It didn't sound good, the way she said it.

"You should give it a try sometime, Rita."

I could see it coming before she opened her mouth, like smoke out of a volcano before it blows. "Zack, don't you even start—"

"Okay, fine. I'm sorry." He threw his hands up in a kind of surrender. He had big hands, with long, thin fingers. I liked them. I wanted to go for another ride with him on his motorcycle, and I felt cheated, because last time I didn't appreciate it enough. "Forget I mentioned it."

He turned to walk down the street. I wanted to run after him, to say something. But I wasn't sure what to say. I had always acted like I didn't like him, even after I sort of did, so what was I supposed to say to change that now, all of a sudden? I wanted to give him a big hug, but nothing moved. It was like an invisible wall on the street between us. I had no idea how to break it down.

"I missed you, Zack." I called it out after him.

He turned around and smiled in a way that made me feel like a kid. Which I usually didn't. Feel like a kid, that is.

"Just keep coming back to these meetings, Sport."

He got on his bike and kick-started it, and I stood there like a jerk watching him ride away. It made me kind of sick, like that night he left our house forever. I felt like some part of me, like my guts, were trying to follow him down the street. And getting all strung out.

When I got back to the car my mom's face was really cold. I mean, it was scary. And I'm not usually scared of her. She drove us home without saying a word. The silence was so heavy and weird I almost would have liked it better if we'd talked.

When we got in I went straight to my room.

I lay on my bed wishing Bill were here, so I could tell him about seeing Zack again. Then I got to wondering if Bill felt all okay again, or if his ribs still hurt, and if he knew I never meant to hurt him.

I took the quart of gin out from under my bed, and I was about to take a few slugs. I'd stolen it from Mom, and she either didn't notice or didn't care. Or wasn't even brave enough to call me on it. I figured it didn't matter if I had a little drink every now and then, because I wasn't an alcoholic like people thought, and I didn't have Bill to take care of, and no one would know anyway.

But then I got scared about having to call tomorrow to see if I had to show up for random testing. If my number came up and I pulled a dirty test, I could get sent to juvenile hall to serve the sentence I was only doing probation for now.

So I put it back under the bed and tried to go to sleep. And just lay there, feeling all those raw nerves. Thinking I'd forgotten how much life feels like sandpaper. And how much I hate to feel.

After a while I fell asleep, and I had this dream that I was leading a meeting and talking about how I could have killed my brother Bill by driving drunk. I woke up with a jump, like in a dream where you're falling.

I couldn't get back to sleep. I kept thinking, Yeah, but I didn't kill him. He's okay. I kept thinking, Bill's okay. I kept thinking, It's only a dream. But I never got back to sleep.

CHAPTER 8

Broken People

It was ten days before I saw Zack in another meeting. Ten long, rotten days. I sat beside him right away. I smiled at him. I wanted to say hi but the word got stuck, like when I tried out for glee club in seventh grade. I kept opening my mouth but I couldn't get started. It was mortifying.

He said, "How you doin', Sport?"

I wished he wouldn't call me that. I wished he wouldn't treat me like a tomboy kid. Even though I sort of was. Only in another way I sort of wasn't anymore, and I wanted Zack to notice. With anybody else I doubt I would have cared.

I didn't hear one word anybody said in the meeting, because I was sitting next to Zack and that was all I could think about. And even when I wasn't thinking about it, I could feel him sitting right there. And it felt good, but also weird, because I wasn't used to feeling anything at all, except that awful scratch of life on my bare, raw nerves. And I was so used to that, I hardly felt it, because it felt normal. A very bad normal.

Truthfully, though, I never much listened to the people in the meeting anyway. They were old. Except for Zack. If you didn't factor Zack in, their average age was probably something like forty or fifty. They had nothing to say to me. And I got my court card signed whether I listened or not. So I just sat there and tried to get real small and stay that way so nobody would think I wanted to talk.

After the meeting I tried to follow him to the door, but it didn't work out so good. He was standing around talking to this older guy, and I was leaning on the wall, thinking he'd be done in a minute, but then I got stuck behind three women who were taking up all the space between the table and the wall. With my crutches I needed more space.

I kept saying, "Excuse me. Excuse me." But they were talking and they didn't hear. Maybe I didn't say it loud enough. It's always hard for me to say something at a time like that, and sometimes when I do it comes out too small.

When I finally got around them I couldn't see where Zack had gone. I headed for the door, figuring I'd look around out front. I ran into Pat before I could get there.

"Hey, Cynnie," she said. "I'm glad to see you keep coming back. How are things at home?"

I was all ready to say, Not now, Pat. Full volume and big. For some reason I thought I could do that.

But then she said, "If you start feeling like you're ready for a sponsor, I'd be happy to help."

I still wasn't sure what that meant. I'd heard people talk about calling their sponsor, or advice their sponsor had given them, but I'd never cared enough to ask.

She started to say something else, but I couldn't wait. I was half watching the open door, and I saw Zack slip by outside.

"Thanks," I said, and took off after him, as fast as you can take off on crutches. "Zack," I called, and everybody on the street turned around.

Zack stopped and waited for me. "Yeah, Sport?"

This is easy, I told myself. You know Zack. Just talk to him. Like he was your friend, which he was. Just talk to him like you used to. This is really easy. But it didn't feel easy. I opened my mouth and it was like glee club tryouts all over again.

"Yeah, what is it, Sport? I gotta get back to work."

"Uh, Zack. I. Uh. Would you . . . ?"

"What, Sport? Would I what?"

"Would you help me fix my tree house?" I didn't know I was about to say that. But I knew I missed my tree house. Life had been looking real bad from the ground floor.

"Well, I guess, but . . . I don't think your mom would take to that so good. Having me come over."

"Come in the afternoon. She's so drunk by then, she won't even notice."

Something came over his face. That little quick second

when you get to see inside somebody, all the way in to a place that hurts. I guess he didn't know, until I said so, that her drinking had gotten so bad. I'd forgotten that my mom was somebody Zack used to care about. I didn't much like having to remember. That was a very weird moment, suddenly having to think about how there was once a Mom and Zack.

"Yeah, okay," he said. "Maybe. I work on weekdays. But maybe Saturday. Yeah. Saturday afternoon. I guess. Wait a minute. How can you even get up there with that big cast on your leg?"

Then I felt really stupid. My face felt hot, and I really hoped that didn't mean it was getting red. "Oh yeah. Well . . ." I couldn't believe he'd just said he would come over Saturday, and now he was about to take it back again. "Maybe for when the cast comes off."

"Okay," he said. "Sometime between now and then. I'll help you make sure the tree house is ready."

I felt like he'd just said "never" or "in your next lifetime."

"Maybe you could take me for another ride on your motorcycle. That was so much fun last time."

"With that big old cast on your leg?"

"Why not?"

He frowned. "I'm not so sure. Anyway, the bike is running bad. I have to tear it all apart and put new bearings in the bottom end. It'll be all over my garage. Maybe when I'm done working on it."

"I could help you." I felt like I was grasping at straws now. But I couldn't help it. I felt like if he got away this time, he might be gone for good, or at least for a long time, something that felt like forever, like last time.

"Pretty technical work, Sport."

"I meant just hand you tools and stuff."

He was still frowning. Like he was trying to find a way to say no. And I thought, you still like me, don't you, Zack? We're friends, right? We're alike, you and me. But I couldn't ask. I couldn't. What if he answered? What if it turned out he was all fixed now and didn't want to be around somebody like me?

"I guess," he said. "Yeah, why not? Saturday."

He gave me his address and I borrowed a pen from one of the meeting people and wrote it down on my hand.

When I got home there was a letter from Nanny and Grampop on my bed. Mom had left it there, I guess.

It was my picture of Bill, with a little note. He was standing up in his playpen, hanging on to the side. Smiling into the camera. He looked really happy.

It made this little knot in my stomach.

I was thinking it was pretty nice of them to send me a picture after everything that happened. And he looked fine, too, not like he was hurt. But then I got to wondering when they actually sent it, so I looked at the postmark, and it was almost six weeks old.

I found my mom looking out the window in the living room.

"What the hell have you been doing with this?" She jumped a mile. "Why didn't you show this to me?"

"I didn't know it was for you."

"Like hell you didn't. You must've known when you opened it. It says Cynnie right on top of the letter."

"I didn't read it," she said. I just waited. I started wondering what else I could do with my life if I could get back all the time I spent waiting for my mom to finish her thoughts. Maybe learn a musical instrument or something. "Usually when she writes, it's to give me advice. It's getting hard to take."

"I'm sure you *don't* take it," I said, but under my breath. She never took any advice from anybody as far as I could tell.

"What did you say?"

"Nothing."

I locked myself back in my room and stared at the picture some more. Trying to think why it made me feel so weird inside. Something about the fact that he looked so . . . happy. But I wanted him to be happy. Right?

But I didn't want to think he was getting along fine without me.

Then I thought, What a terrible thing to think. What kind of sister are you? What, you want him to be miserable? No. Maybe. I don't know.

I just didn't want to think maybe he forgot all about me.

This is the point at which I would've gone to Kiki's. If I could've. I would tell her I had a date. Borrow her makeup. Maybe look in her closet for something to wear.

Instead I went up to the attic and plowed through her boxes.

When she left home it was kind of sudden. She left a bunch of stuff behind, clothes and stuff. A curling iron that didn't work when it didn't feel like it. Some old makeup. When it came to makeup, Kiki had everything. I've seen people stockpiling supplies for the great earthquake who don't keep so many spares of things around. I'd boxed it all up and taken it to the attic so I wouldn't miss her so much. I tried extra hard not to miss her now.

I weeded out a couple of dresses and a slightly dry tube of mascara. And tweezers. Then I shoved everything back in the boxes and got downstairs as fast as I could. I felt like the attic was haunted. Like my sister was a ghost. I didn't know I missed her so much.

I looked at myself in the mirror. I knew this wasn't what I wanted to look like, and I didn't have much time to change it. I plucked a few stray eyebrow hairs. I knew I was definitely in love, even though I never had been before, because nothing short of love would make a person do something that hurts as much as plucking your eyebrows. It made my eyes water, and the skin where I'd been plucking looked all red. I got an ice cube and rubbed it on the red places. Then I tried to figure out how to put on the mascara.

The dresses were all too big. But that wasn't really the problem. When I put on one of Kiki's dresses I felt like somebody else, somebody I never meant to be. Like if you know something doesn't fit in a space, and you just fold it over and squish it in anyway. I decided I'd wear some makeup and dress as myself. Zack would just have to like me for me.

I sat on the back stoop, waiting for it to be afternoon. The minutes went so slow it was silly. It was a warm day, and my leg started to itch under my cast. Then I rubbed my eye and got worried I might've smeared the makeup, so I went in the house to look.

Mom was passed out on the couch with a cigarette butt burning in her hand. The living room smelled like burned filter. I slipped it out of her fingers and squashed it in the ashtray.

I went into the bathroom and looked in the mirror, and I had a black eye from rubbing the mascara. I had to clean it all off and start over again. This grown-up woman thing was hard. And weird. I mean, how are you even supposed to rub your eye?

On my way back through the living room I saw the bottle on the coffee table. Mom's gin. I almost had a slug, to settle my nerves. Then I thought, I can't go over to Zack's smelling like I've been drinking. He's in the program now. He might think badly of me.

I never once thought about how it would blow my probation. Nothing really mattered now except going over to Zack's.

He had half the bike engine all apart on newspapers on the garage floor. I leaned on the wall, trying to look casual. I had Kiki's mascara in my pocket, in case I forgot and rubbed my eye. It dug into my hip, but I didn't move.

I forgot I was supposed to be handing him tools.

He was lying on his side, kind of half under the bike, and some of his hair spilled off onto the newspaper. It looked almost blond. Who knew, when it was only half an inch long, that it would grow out almost blond?

Because he wasn't looking at me, I thought I could say something. But I had no idea what it should be.

I said, "What's a sponsor?"

He sat up. Picked up a shop towel and wiped off the wrench and his hands. He looked right at me, which made it harder to have a conversation. I remembered the conversations we used to have. They were so easy. Why couldn't it be that way now?

He said, "Somebody in the program who works with you, kind of more one on one. Helps you figure out the program when you get stuck. And you can call them if you think you want to drink. Or even if you just need someone to talk to. And they help you work the steps. Which can be kind of confusing at first."

"So how do you know who your sponsor is?"

"You just ask somebody."

"Will *you* be my sponsor?"

I knew there was nobody else I could stand to have except him.

He kept looking right at me. I was getting dizzy, waiting for him to answer. I was starting to think that if the answer was yes, he would have said it by now. He had that look on his face, like when I asked to come over here today. Like he wanted to say no.

"That's good that you're ready for one." I didn't know if that meant yes, but I couldn't ask. "But not me, though."

"Why not?"

"Two reasons. I've only got sixty days. You need someone with more time."

"Sixty days! That's, like, two months! That's tons of time."

"Not really, Sport." He was looking at me real hard. It made me squirm inside. "The other reason is more important. Women are supposed to have women sponsors. Or girls. You know what I mean. And men have men sponsors."

"Why? What's the difference?"

"Let me see. How do I explain it? That sponsor relationship, you have to keep it real simple. Not get it mixed up with other things. Other feelings. Know what I mean?"

"Yeah. I guess." I guess I was getting that—how things can get so complicated with somebody like Zack. But it scared me, too, because it made me think again that maybe he didn't want to be around me anymore. Because maybe we weren't alike the way we used to be. I said, "Zack? Now that you're in the program . . . are you . . . fixed?"

He looked at me like he had no idea what I was talking about. It was like he'd forgotten that whole conversation we had. How could he forget that? It felt like the most important thing that had ever happened to me.

"What do you mean, fixed?"

"You used to say we were broken, remember?"

"Oh. Well, it's only been sixty days, Sport. It doesn't happen quite so fast. I'm just not acting quite as stupid and crazy now. It's like I'm the same person but I don't always act on my first impulse."

"So you're just *trying* to be fixed." Which was bad enough. That already broke the pact.

"I'm just saying I'm a little better. Why?"

"I was worried that now I'm the only one."

He sat there sort of chewing on his lip for a minute. That's when I figured out there was no easy answer for that one. Or if there was, he didn't know it, either.

After a while he said, "Why don't you try the program, too? What've you got to lose?"

I felt like I could lose everything, but I wasn't sure how to explain. I felt like I could lose *me*. What if I woke up and something had fixed me, made me whole again? Made me so I didn't even want to do crazy shit? Who would I be? I sure as hell wouldn't be me. But I didn't know how to explain all that to Zack.

So I said, "It's a total mistake that I even have to go there. That car accident had nothing to do with drinking. I hadn't even had that much. It was about wanting to drive fast. Just because . . . Well, *you* know why. You told me yourself. You said it makes you feel whole for just a minute. So I wanted to try it. This whole AA thing is a mistake. But I couldn't say all that in court. How could I?"

Zack was looking at me funny. Like I was talking in a foreign language or something. "Cynnie—"

"You don't think I'm an alcoholic, do you, Zack?" I thought if he said he did, I would just die.

"Nobody gets to decide that for somebody else. You are if you say you are. Let's say you're not. It was all a big mistake. You really have nothing to lose by working the steps. Right?"

Except that I wouldn't be me anymore. But I think I loved that crazy me so much because Zack was there to share it with me. Now that he'd turned his back on it, I wasn't sure how much I even cared. Maybe this "me" thing wasn't even worth hanging on to.

"Now, my mother," I said, "she could really use it."

The minute the words came out of my mouth I regretted them. I forgot Zack actually cared what happened with my mom.

"How 'bout if you give it a try . . . for *me?*" he said after a minute.

The only reason he could possibly have given me that I couldn't ignore.

When I woke up the next morning I lay in bed for a while, feeling like I couldn't move. Well, maybe like a cross between couldn't and didn't want to. It was like that feeling I had when I knew they were going to take Bill away. Like you're a sailing ship scooting along on the water, but then all of a sudden there's no wind.

And I wasn't thinking much, either. It was like all the thoughts I could think were bad ones. But I do remember thinking that if I saw Pat at the meeting that evening, I'd ask her to be my sponsor. Partly because of the promise I'd made to Zack. Partly because when things like this happened, like not being able to move, I wanted to feel like there was somebody or something to help me with them.

Then I thought how nice it would be to have one of those mothers who came in and pulled you out of bed and helped you get dressed and handed you a nice packed lunch and made sure you got out the door on time.

But I didn't. Which made having a sponsor sound like an even better idea.

I was nearly half an hour late for school because I couldn't break the spell. No matter how hard I tried, I just couldn't get any wind into my sails.

I asked Pat if she would drive me home, and she said yeah, she would, so I called my mom and told her not to bother.

"Thanks," I said, while we walked out to her car, which turned out to be an old beater of an Oldsmobile. "This is much safer. To go home with you. My mom is so smashed by this time of night. It scares the hell out of me to drive with her. I swear I'm taking my life into my hands."

I waited in the cold for her to unlock the passenger door and let me in. Then we sat there and she let the engine warm up for a while and ran the heater.

"Sounds like things are bad at home."

I shrugged. "Just the same as they always are."

"And they were always bad. Right?"

I shrugged again. "Hard to know how other people's lives are, you know?"

She looked at me in the dark, like she could look close and see all the things I didn't say. But then all she said was, "Seat belt."

I put it on and we started for home.

After a few blocks I said, "You told me a couple of times you'd be my sponsor. You know. If I was ready for one."

"Are you?"

"I guess. I don't know. I'm ready to work the program for real."

"Good," she said. About time, I thought I heard, even though she didn't say it.

I didn't tell her why I was ready to do it or who I was doing it for. I'm not stupid.

"So what do I do? I mean, if you're gonna be my sponsor."

"I'll give you a book tonight and I want you to read the chapter on the first step."

Ah. See? I knew this would be like school. Sooner or later.

She pulled into my driveway. We sat there for a while with the motor running. I was glad the house was there, all in one piece. I always expected my mom to burn it down or blow it up while I was away. But I never really knew I was thinking that until I saw it in one piece again.

Pat said, "So, you got a mother, but she's usually drunk."

"More like always."

"Father?"

"He died a long time ago. I only just barely remember him."

"Friends?"

"I had a couple. A while ago. But I chased one off, and the other, I don't know where he is anymore." And the best friend I ever had ran out on me, but now I found him again, but he's not really acting much like my friend anymore. But she knew Zack, and like I said, I'm not stupid. "And I had a kid brother. He was my friend."

"Did he die?"

"No, my grandparents came and took him away. Because my mom didn't look after him right."

"What about *you*? Why'd they leave *you*?"

"That's what I wanted to know." Then, after a minute, I said, "Everybody always does. Anyway."

I could see her nodding a little in the dark. "Never really had a chance, did ya?"

That made me a little uneasy, so I took off my seat belt and got out. She had to lean over and close the door because it was sticky. She had to pull it hard from the inside. I couldn't swing it hard enough to make it catch.

I walked up the driveway in the dark. In the cold. Wishing she hadn't reminded me how much I'm on my own in the world.

"Cynnie." I turned around, and she had her window down and her head stuck out, talking to me. "You forgot the book."

Oh yeah. My homework. God forbid I should forget my homework. Like I don't get enough at school.

Just as I was taking the book out of her hands, she said, "Call me every day."

"And say what?"

" 'Hello' would be a good start. After that we'll just wing it."

When I got inside, my mom was nearly passed out on the sofa. I mean, her eyes were open, and her head was nodding around a little. But she sort of looked in my direction, and you could

109

tell she had no idea who or what she was looking at, so that qualifies as passed out as far as I'm concerned. It's close enough. She had an empty bottle of something on the coffee table in front of her, and a full ashtray, and a cigarette in her fingers that was all burned down into the filter. But at least it had gone out on its own, before she burned the house down. The smell was nasty.

I walked right up to her and stood over her, and she looked up at me, and you could see her trying to focus. "What if Pat hadn't driven me home? You were going to come get me like this? In this condition?"

"I waited all night," she said. Or something like that. It was really pathetic how one word ran into the next. "I didn't get going until you called."

I just shook my head at her. Nobody could get that drunk in ten or fifteen minutes. I'm sure she had plenty after I called. But to get where she was now, you'd need a good running head start. I took three of her cigarettes out of the pack on the table. Right in front of her. She never said a word. I'm not sure she even saw.

I sat outside on the patio in the dark and smoked all three in a row. I was looking up at my tree house, thinking how much it sucked to get stuck on the ground for all this time. I was trying not to think this other thing, but in my gut it was there, and I couldn't ignore it. I was jealous of my mom. Because she didn't have to do all this work. She didn't have to go to school, and then probation, and she didn't have to go without even one little drink to take the edge off, because nobody was going to test her pee. She didn't have to have a sponsor telling her what to do. She didn't even have to try. And she didn't. She just did what was easiest.

I crushed out the cigarette butts on the patio and left them there for her to clean up some other time.

CHAPTER 9

Don't You Dare

That next Saturday morning, Pat met me at the IHOP for breakfast, which I guess was pretty nice of her, and then to even it out she insisted on talking about the steps.

"How're you doing on step one?" she asked. She put tons and tons of Tabasco sauce on her scrambled eggs. It made my mouth hurt just to look at her.

I'd been doing my best all week not to think about step one. In fact, I'd even managed not to read the stuff in the book about it. I heard them say the short version of the steps at the beginning of every meeting, but I swear they didn't even make any sense. "Okay, I guess."

"Do you understand it?"

"Um . . ."

"Trouble with the first part? Or the second part?"

I just stared at her, trying to figure out how to fake my way out of this one. I didn't even remember it had two parts.

She set down her fork and looked at me funny. "You didn't even read it."

"I forget it now."

The waitress came by to refill Pat's coffee cup. Pat put away a lot of coffee.

Usually I felt sorry for waitresses. It seems like they've got a rotten job. But right about then I wanted to trade with her. I could hang up pancake orders for the cooks, and she could hear all about step one.

"When this breakfast is over," she said, "so is this sponsorship arrangement between you and me."

First I wanted to stomp out, but I still had bacon on my plate. I love bacon. And also there was the part about Zack. I was doing this for Zack. "*Why?* What the hell did *I* do?" I felt stung. Seriously stung. Which was weird, because I hardly even liked Pat. But I couldn't get why all my relationships with everybody I ever met kept turning out the same. I thought a sponsor was supposed to help you. Be on your side. For a change.

"Nothing. That's just it. You haven't done anything. You haven't even said you're an alcoholic. You haven't admitted your life is unmanageable. And when I give you the simplest little thing to do, like call me on the phone, like read a step, you don't even bother. I can't recover *for* you, Cynnie. I can hand you things, but you gotta take it from me. You gotta grab on."

I looked out the window and watched a man buy a newspaper out of a coin-operated box. I wondered what Bill was doing this morning. I wondered if Zack would come to the noon meeting. I never answered Pat. She'd already made up her mind about me.

After a while I started to worry whether she meant what she said about when breakfast was over. She was shoveling those eggs in awful fast, like she couldn't wait to be done and get out of my life for good. Like everybody else.

So I said, "I'll do something. I'll tell you something. Aren't you supposed to tell your sponsor things?" She just looked at me and waited, so I kept going. "When I wake up in the morning these past few days, I can't move. I mean, I guess I could. But I can't make myself. Like my body is maybe three hundred pounds and that's more than I can lift. And it's kind of scary. Because it feels like it's bigger than me, and there's nothing I can do. And it goes on like that for about half an hour. Sometimes more. If I had a real mother, she'd come drag me out of bed and tell me I'm late for school. Which I always am. But I don't, so I have to fix this myself. And it feels like . . ." This was the part I didn't know how to say, because I didn't even really get it myself. "It's like it has something to do with the fact that there's a day out there. You know. Waiting for me. It's like there's a wall between me and the day and I can't figure out how to get through it. Or maybe I don't even want to."

I stopped and waited, but Pat didn't say anything. Her look

hadn't softened up much, either. She was almost done with her food.

I said, "Isn't that the sort of thing you're supposed to tell your sponsor?"

"What do you think it means?"

"I have no idea. That's why I asked *you*."

"Sounds like you're having a bout of depression. Or even panic attacks."

I shook my head. Way off base. I was disappointed. "No. I don't feel depressed. Or scared."

"That you know of," she said.

"What does *that* mean?"

"I don't think you feel much of anything anymore."

"How can you say that? I feel things."

"Maybe. Maybe some things. The really big ones. Most people, by the time they get to this program, they're so out of touch with their emotions, they don't even *know* what they feel. Takes the emotional equivalent of an atom bomb going off under their chair. Like if they're scared of something—like a social situation—they'll say it bores them. And they believe it. Later things sort of unfreeze and then they look back and see where they were all along."

She gave a little signal to the waitress and the woman caught it right away and brought a little paper receipt that I guess was the check.

I said, "So, are you still my sponsor?"

She hit me with a look I really hated. Like she was study-ing something fascinating written on the inside of the back of

115

my head. "Cynnie," she said, "do you even think you have a problem?"

I couldn't answer, because I couldn't give her the answer she wanted. And I couldn't lie with her looking right through me like that.

"I don't think I can help you," she said, and got up to go.

I sat there with my face burning, which I guess meant it was turning red. Even my ears were burning. After a second I got up and ran after her.

She was halfway across the parking lot, almost to her car, when I yelled out her name. "Pat!"

She stopped and turned around. But she didn't come any closer. Just waited to see what I had. What did I have?

All of a sudden I was pissed. I mean, really, really pissed. I felt *that*, all right. Whatever else I could or couldn't feel, I sure felt furious right then. My hands were all balled up in fists down at my sides, and I could feel my fingernails cutting into my palms. And I had to work to keep from crying, because I always cry when I get that frustrated and mad. And I had to yell at the top of my lungs, because she was halfway across the parking lot, and if I didn't say it fast, I was scared she'd be in her car and gone.

"Don't you give up on me!" I screamed. A bunch of people on the street turned and stared. "Don't you dare give up on me!" Don't you frigging dare.

She started to walk back toward where I was standing.

My palms stung from where my fingernails were digging in, but I couldn't unclench my fists.

"My own mother doesn't even care enough to try with me. My own grandparents left me behind like I was something that wasn't even important enough to bother packing. Even my sister ditched me because I wasn't worth having to talk to my mom." And then Zack deserted me, but I couldn't bring myself to tell her that. She was getting closer now, and I was losing my fight with crying. I could feel tears squeeze out no matter how hard I tried to hold them. And when I talked, it bent my mouth around funny. "I have no friends. I asked you to be my sponsor. And your sponsor is supposed to be the one person who doesn't just blow you off."

She was almost nose to nose with me by now. I could feel her breath on my face. It smelled like hot sauce.

"Don't give up on me," I said. Quiet now. Like I finally realized it was a sad thing to have to say.

Then I waited. And waited. And waited.

"Tell you what," she said at last. "If *you* don't give up on you, I won't, either. Have we got a deal?"

I sniffled and wiped my nose on my sleeve. Which is gross, I know, but so is what would've happened if I hadn't. Then I nodded.

I felt her hand slap down on the top of my head. Not really hard, but hard enough. Enough to surprise me, like I might've just been smacked a little. But then she gave the top of my head a couple of pats and walked off.

And I stood there, trying not to cry. Wondering why I'd just let somebody—anybody—matter to me. And, worse yet, let them know about it.

⁙ ⁙ ⁙

When I got home I called Nanny and Grampop. Nanny answered. My heart was pounding, wondering what she'd say to me. We hadn't talked since the accident.

I said, "I want to talk to Bill."

Nanny said, "Talk . . . to Bill?" Like that was totally impossible or something. I was still waiting for her to say something about "It." I forgot this was *my* family. We only talk about easy things. About the things that hardly matter.

"Yeah. Talk to Bill."

"He doesn't do a lot of talking, Cynthia."

"Well, he can listen. He understands me. And he can say my name. Just put him on the phone, would you?"

A long silence. I hate grown-ups. "I don't even know if he'll hold it."

"Well, just hold it up to his ear, will you, Nanny? When he hears my voice, he'll listen." My fuse was getting kind of short and we could both hear it.

"Okay, we'll try it."

"Bill," I said. "Bill, Bill, Bill, Bill, Bill."

Finally he said it. "Thynnie."

I almost started to cry. But I couldn't let that happen. I couldn't give in to it. I had something important to do. Besides, I'd cried plenty enough for one day.

I sang him a couple of songs. The first was just the alphabet song, because I couldn't think of anything. Then I sang some Christmas carols, and I could hear him sort of humming, singing along with me.

Then, just when I said, "Cynnie loves you, Bill, you know that, right?" Nanny got back on the line and said that was all the phone holding she could do for one time. "Fine," I said. "But don't be surprised if I call back tomorrow."

I started calling Bill every day. Usually after I got home from school, because it was late enough in the afternoon, my mom wasn't really a factor. I thought I'd really hit on a way to make life livable again. I didn't even care that Nanny sighed real big and dramatic every time she heard it was me. I could almost hear her rolling her eyes on the other end of the line. I didn't care. She could think or say or roll whatever she wanted. I practically had Bill back.

Zack came over to fix my tree house. With another guy. I couldn't believe it. This was not the way it was supposed to go at all. I had it all planned out in my head. With no other guy. It was like I'd gotten hit with something. I stood there feeling my face burn. Didn't he know it was important to be able to talk to him alone?

They were leaning this long ladder up against my tree. I didn't see Zack's motorcycle. Just an old beat-up gray Chevy at the curb. I took a big breath and walked up to them.

Zack said, "Hiya, Sport. This is Earl. He's a friend of Bill W., too."

I said, "Huh?" Which is, like, always a stupid thing to say, no matter where you put it in a conversation. I said, "What do you mean? I don't know any Bill W. You don't mean my brother Bill, right? Because he's not a 'W.' "

They both laughed. I looked at Earl and thought I remembered seeing him at some meetings.

"Bill Wilson, the AA founder. If you want to know if somebody's in the program, you ask if they're a friend of Bill W. It's a little more discreet than saying, 'Hey, are you an alcoholic?' "

I said, "Oh, I get it." I wanted Earl to be gone. I wanted to be alone with Zack. I didn't want to be a friend of Bill W. Any guy who invented that stupid program, I didn't even want to know him. But then I remembered again that I had to think different about the program because I promised Zack I'd try. I tried to breathe. My brain wasn't working fast enough.

I said, "Where's your motorcycle, Zack? Is it still all apart?"

"Yeah. Turns out I gotta rebuild the whole bottom end. But I'm nearly done."

He was holding the ladder for Earl, who was halfway up it with a two-by-six. He was knocking the board with a hammer, trying to get it to wedge between the tree trunk and the right-hand side of my tree house to hold the whole deal up.

I couldn't think of anything more to say to Zack, with Earl right where he could hear, so I hobbled over to the porch and sat down. I thought about the day Richie and Snake and I built that tree house, with Zack sitting on the porch watching, just the reverse of how we were now. And I thought about Snake again. Like, where was he right this minute? Was he okay? But I didn't get to think too long or too hard because it didn't take them long to finish.

They walked over to where I was sitting. Earl said that ought to do 'er, she'd be pretty strong now. That's how he talked. Called a tree house "she." Zack asked when I'd get my cast off, and I told him not soon enough.

Then Earl was tying the ladder onto the roof of his ratty old car. Zack was just standing there. I thought, Talk, Cynnie. Spit it out. In a minute he'll be gone.

I put a lot of force behind it and it popped out. "It's actually a week from Tuesday."

"What is?"

"That I get my cast off. You promised me a ride on your bike, remember?"

He got a funny look on his face, like he was trying to remember promising. Actually, I'm not sure he did promise. I know we talked about it.

"Yeah," he said. "I guess."

It wasn't quite what I wanted. Which would've been something more like, "Perfect, I can't wait." But it was enough. It had to be.

One of the days after that, I got home from school and my mom was sitting up at the kitchen table. Really not passed out at all. It was unfortunate. She didn't look very happy, either. I pictured her like this cartoon character with a dark black cloud hanging over her head. Maybe with lightning bolts shooting through it.

"Why have you been calling Nanny and Grampop?"

I got a little pissy about the stern business. Don't start pulling that "I'm the boss" crap on me. If you're the boss, act like the boss. All the time. "Because I feel like it."

She held up a couple of papers that I figured must be the phone bill. Waved them around. Always the actress. "You spent forty-seven dollars of our money talking about me with them. What are you telling them? Are you planning something behind my back?"

From the tone of her voice, I don't think she was guessing surprise party. More like family intervention kind of a thing.

"I don't talk about you to Nanny and Grampop."

"Bullshit! Then why are you calling them? You never talk to them! You don't even like them!"

"True enough," I said. "I call Bill."

She gave me the evil eye. "I don't believe you. Bill doesn't even talk."

"Would everybody please stop saying that?" I was shouting all of a sudden. "He's not a dog, for God's sake. He understands things. He communicates."

She sat back and folded her arms over her ratty, lumpy robe. "So why don't you tell me what you two talk about? Forty-seven dollars' worth?"

"Nothing. I just talk to him. We sing songs and stuff."

She laughed the way people do when they're not happy and nothing is funny. "Not for forty-seven dollars you don't. This stops now."

"Like hell it does."

"Unless you want to pay these bills yourself."

Then I walked out because I was seriously about to say something that would have been going too far even for me. I mean, I actually had to leave before something really bad happened, and I caused it.

I called Nanny and Grampop's house collect. She accepted the charges.

"What's wrong?" she asked, sounding out of breath. "Is it your mother? What happened?"

"Nothing happened. I called to talk to Bill."

Long silence on the line. "Collect?"

"Mom's pissed off about paying for the calls."

"And you think Grampop will like it any better?"

"Just this once, Nanny, please?"

She sighed and held the phone for Bill.

The next day I called again, but not collect. I didn't care what my mother thought. In fact, I didn't care what my mother thought every day for the whole rest of the month.

The day I got my cast off, Zack took me for that ride I'd been begging for. The bike was sounding real good since he'd done all that work on it, real loud and strong.

I put my arms around him, and he said, "Where to, Sport?"

It seemed so obvious, I couldn't believe he would ask. "The reservoir, of course."

"Sure you don't want to see something new?"

"Positive." I wanted it to be just like it was before. I wanted everything to be just like it was before.

I held him real tight, waiting for that moment when he put on the gas and nearly blasted me right off the back of the bike. But he accelerated nice and smooth and never got more than five miles over the speed limit the whole way.

It was tragic.

Zack tried skipping stones on the reservoir, but he was pathetic. I mean, I hate to say it, because it was Zack and all, but really. Pathetic. I tried to teach him, but it's one of those things you have to practice about a million times. And he wasn't relaxed like last time so I didn't figure we would be there that long.

"How're you getting along with Pat as a sponsor?" he asked when he had pretty much embarrassed himself and given up.

I made a noise that came out like an old engine that doesn't want to start. "Okay. I guess. Sometimes. I mean . . . sometimes I'm not sure if she's on my side or not."

"She is," he said.

"How do you know?"

"Trust me on this one."

After that it got a little sticky, what to talk about. So I said, "If you were me, and you needed a job to earn extra money but you were only fourteen, what would you do?"

I was really hoping he would have an actual idea. Like maybe he even had some work that needed doing or something. Or knew someone in the program who did, someone I

halfway knew. Because the idea of going out and getting working papers and asking total strangers for a job—wow. I kept
trying that on but I could never really get it to fit. No matter
how I looked at it, it still sucked.

"Hmmm," he said. "Hmmm. When I was your age I used to
knock on neighbors' doors and ask if I could mow their lawns
or split firewood or if they had any odd jobs."

That was almost a worse fit than getting working papers
and answering ads. Who could bring themselves to do that?
Knock on total strangers' doors? We didn't know any of our
neighbors. Why would we? They didn't want anything to do
with us and I didn't blame them. There was just no way. Mom
would have to keep paying for the calls, like it or not.

Then there was nothing left to talk about at all, and I got
scared he'd pack it up. Like, Okay, too awkward, let's go. Not
that he would say it like that, but I'd know. So I tried telling
him something honest. Same as I did with Pat that day in the
restaurant. Hoping if I was honest, it would be harder to blow
me off.

I said, "There's one thing about this whole working with a
sponsor bit. . . . What if I make all these changes, and then . . .
Who am I going to be if I can't be me anymore?"

He laughed. I was so surprised. And hurt. "Why is that
funny?"

"I'm sorry, Cynnie. I wasn't laughing at you. You know
that, right? It's just that . . . It's like, we should all be so lucky
that you'd change that much. It's just . . . so incredibly slow
and difficult."

"Gee, thanks. I feel so much better now."

"I'm sorry. If you hang around, you'll get what I mean. We better head back."

And then that was it, it was all over except the ride home. And it wasn't anything like last time. I should've known. Nothing is ever anything like last time.

When I got home, I called Pat. I didn't tell her about seeing Zack. But I told her about calling Bill, and how my mom didn't want to pay for it anymore. And how I'd been thinking about maybe getting a job, but that sounded like a terrible idea, too.

She said after a while I would figure out which sounded better, not having to work or not getting to call Bill. She said I didn't have to decide today, which was a relief. I was thinking maybe this sponsor thing wasn't so bad. I figured Zack was right about Pat.

"What'd you do today?" she asked.

"Nothing much. Just been around the house all day."

Then she hit me with it. She said, "I want to talk to you about Zack."

My stomach got all icy really fast. "What about him?"

"If you'd said you went for a ride on his motorcycle today, maybe there'd be nothing to talk about. But you just lied to me, so I expect we have a problem. He's a grown man, first of all. And you're a fourteen-year-old girl. And if you're trying to get him to cross a line, you're doing a bad thing for both of you. It's really important not to start any new relationships or make any big changes in your first year. And that's even with somebody your own age."

I couldn't believe what I was hearing. I was outraged. I never used that word before so far as I know, but boy, that really says it. "Were you spying on me?"

"Hardly. I got better things to do. I was coming out of the hardware store when you two went buzzing by. Care to tell me why you felt you had to lie about it?"

"This is none of your business."

"Look. There's a very unflattering name we have for any guy in the program who would take advantage of a newcomer—just when they're most vulnerable—and it's the business of any other member to gently remind that guy how it'd be the wrong thing to do. I already talked to Zack and he seems to be in a good place with it, but I'm warning you—out of caring for you, Cynnie—I'm seeing trouble here. Either way."

I was so tied up in a knot, I could hardly answer. "You . . . talked to Zack? You talked to Zack . . . about me? Oh, my God. How could you do that? You had no right. You had no right to do that. I can't believe that."

I know she said a couple more things. I remember her voice sounding really flat and even. Just the opposite of mine.

Then I hung up on her.

I climbed up into my tree house for the first time since the accident and sat there fuming. I didn't know where she got off. I didn't know what to do to feel better again. But one thing I knew for damn sure. I was never talking to Pat again. Never, not as long as I lived.

❖ ❖ ❖

The day after that, my mom and I had this incredible fight. The kind where you feel like it's picking you up and carrying you along with it, like a tornado, and you start feeling like the fight is in control, like it's a real thing, it's bigger than you, and you couldn't stop it if you tried.

It all started when I tried to call Bill, but I couldn't make the phone dial the number. It came on with this weird fast busy signal before I even finished dialing.

My mom was in the kitchen, eating some leftover something right out of the casserole dish.

"There's something wrong with the phone," I said.

She didn't even look up at me. Just looked right into that goop she was eating and said, "Only if you're trying to call long distance. I had it blocked."

"You *what?*" It came out like this shriek, and then I was already in that part of the thing that takes over for you. Suddenly I knew what people meant when they said they hit the ceiling. I felt like some force, like steam escaping, was going to send me straight up in the air until I banged my head.

"I told you, Cynthia. I told you we couldn't afford this. We only have your father's Social Security and—"

"Oh yeah? *Why* do we only have that? Why don't you work at a job like normal people? You're not sick. Your arms aren't broken. Why don't you work and take care of us, so we have money for basic stuff like calling my little brother who got sent away? He's my brother—do you get that? He's your son. Flesh and blood, Mom. He's our flesh and blood. Our *family.*

Does that mean anything to you at all? It's your fault I can't see him, and now you won't even let me talk to him. Because you didn't feel like taking care of him. But you *had* him. So you *have* to. It's your job. Are you going to give me away, too, if I'm too much trouble? Is that what you do when you get tired? Throw your kids away? And tired from what? You don't *do* anything. Except drink. And sleep around."

My throat was starting to hurt from the yelling. She looked up at me, and she didn't even look mad. Her eyes looked empty and dead. It was like she shut down and locked the doors and put out a sign that said "nobody home" so I couldn't get to her. I could see she was going to be this big brick wall, and I was going to bash myself into pieces on her and never hurt her one bit.

All she said was, "You try working for a living and then come back and tell me how easy it is."

"I will. I'll get a part-time job and raise my own money for the phone bill."

"Good. Fine."

"But it sucks. It sucks that I should have to. You're the mother. And you don't do anything. I mean, what do you actually *do?*"

She just got up and wandered off toward her bedroom. She left that nasty casserole sitting out on the table, and I sure wasn't going to put it away for her.

I stomped off—as best you can stomp when you've just gotten a big cast off your broken leg—to the back patio and sat staring up at my tree house. Thinking about going up. But

I felt too shaky. The whole middle of me was shaking, I was so mad. I couldn't believe she fixed it so I couldn't call Bill. My hands were shaking, too. I had to do something to stop feeling like this, but I didn't know what. I actually even thought about calling Pat, but only for a split second.

I went inside and called Zack instead.

He sounded really surprised to hear it was me. "What's up?" he said. I think he could tell that I was upset.

"Can I come over? I need to talk to somebody."

"Oh," he said. "Uh. You should call your sponsor. You should call Pat."

"Please," I said. "Just for a few minutes. I just want to see you and talk to you for a few minutes." I kept it to myself that I was never going to talk to Pat again in my whole life.

"Oh, I . . ." I waited for him to finish, and my stomach started getting lower and heavier, because I could hear him trying to say no. "I can't tonight."

"It'll just be a few minutes."

"I can't tonight, Cynnie. I have a . . ." I waited. I didn't know what else to do. "A . . . you know . . . sort of a date. It's not for a couple of hours, but I just got home from work and I need to get ready."

I could hear this weird buzzing in my ears, like a swarm of invisible bees just outside my head. And my skin felt strange—tingly, like someone threw me in the ocean really suddenly and I was shocked from the cold of it, and my whole body went numb, just like that.

"You should call Pat. That's what she's for."

"Right," I said.

And then I was off the phone, but I couldn't remember if I'd said goodbye or if I'd just hung up. That time was a blank.

I went up to my tree house and got that bottle of gin out from under the mattress where I'd stashed it. No more of this working hard while my mother did nothing. From now on I wouldn't care. Send me to juvie, force me to go to meetings, I don't care. Expel me from school, no big deal. No more caring about anything from this point on. From now on I let everything slide, like my mom does. If she could do it, so could I.

This is the part that might be a little hard to explain. The part where I decided I was going over to Zack's anyway. Maybe "decide" is the wrong way to say it. Maybe it's more like something just pulled me over there. I just know I'd been sitting there sipping on that gin for a long time, and when it hit my gut, it started to warm things up, and then I was more awake inside. Not quite so numb and frozen. And I kept thinking there was still time. He had a date coming, but she wasn't there yet. Once she got there, it would be too late. But right now there was still time. Maybe if I told him how I felt about him. Maybe I could still change the way this all worked out.

The part where it started to sound like a good, right idea— that's the part I still can't really explain.

I changed my clothes first and put on a little makeup, even though I thought I didn't have much time. But also, this had to be perfect, so there was a lot that was important, and I had to try to balance it all, like a juggler with torches that are on fire. I had to get this right. I didn't have dresses or anything, so I just wore this skinny little tank top that didn't cover my whole middle. I even snuck into the bathroom and stole some of my mom's red lipstick.

I walked to Zack's house as fast as I could. It was starting to get dark, and it was cold. I should've worn a jacket. But there was nothing I could do about that, so I walked faster to try to stay warm. Even though my leg was feeling kind of achy.

When I knocked on his door I could feel this pounding in my ears, but it felt far off, like it was happening to somebody else.

He opened the door. He had this big, sweet smile on his face, like he was expecting something wonderful, and when he saw me, his face just fell. He was wearing a sports jacket, and he smelled good, like aftershave.

"Cynnie," he said. Disappointed. "You've been drinking." I was surprised. I didn't think he would know. I didn't think it was that much, that it would show on me that fast and that easy. "You need to call your sponsor. You need to call Pat."

I had no idea what to say, so I just came right into his living room and put my arms around him. Put my head against his chest and smelled his aftershave. I don't think I said anything at all.

He pushed me away. "Cynnie," he said. "My God. You're fourteen years old."

I tried not to let on how much I was feeling stung. "So? My mom was, like, way older than you. We're closer than you two were in our ages."

132

"Yeah, but your mom and me, we were both adults. Cynnie, a guy my age and a fourteen-year-old girl? That's not even legal. It's not even right."

I just stood there with my head down. I felt like I needed a big blanket to wrap up in or something. I felt all exposed.

Zack looked at me like he could hear me think that. "Aren't you cold?" he asked. It sounded like he was accusing me of something. I didn't answer.

Bad news is, he kept talking. "God, Cynnie, look at you. Look what you're turning into. You hate your mom so much. You have no respect for her. You look down on her. Because she drinks too much and she sleeps with a lot of men. And now look at you. If you hate that so much about her, why are you going all those same places yourself?"

Then I remember running down his driveway. I don't remember running out the door. I know I did, but it's a blank. I just remember running as fast as I could.

I ran all the way home. My chest felt like it was about to explode but I kept running. I knew I was hurting my leg but I didn't care. It hurt more and more but I kept running until I was home. I leaned on my tree trying to breathe again. I wasn't thinking anything. I was careful not to think. I wasn't sure how long I could keep that up.

I climbed up above it all. I sat on my mattress and tried to finish the bottle. If I could drink enough, maybe I'd never have to come down. Maybe I could disappear for real. That's all I'd ever wanted, all along. Just to disappear. It really didn't seem like too much to ask. I sat there in the dark, trying to make my mind go blank. Trying to make it this black sea, like a dark night with no moon. I didn't want to think anything at all.

One thought did break through, though. Well, it wasn't a thought, really. It was a feeling. Not the kind Pat said I didn't have. An actual physical feeling. It was the lump of Harvey's pocketknife, pressing against my leg. I was sitting on it.

I opened it out and looked at it as best I could in the dark. I touched the tip of it, and it was still sharp enough to make my finger bleed. I sucked on the end of my finger, and it wasn't that much blood, but enough, and I was really aware of the taste of it.

I thought, You want to disappear? You're a big girl now. You know what that really means. It's not a pretend thing where you close your eyes and wish. If you really want to disappear, you can.

I got outside myself in a weird way then, and thought about what would happen when I had to tell somebody about this later. If there was a later. Like Pat, or whoever that person is in your life that you have to cough up all your secrets for. She'd ask how serious I was.

So, how serious was I?

I could feel that old part of me, the part I'd been trying to leave behind. The real me. The broken me. I could feel it waiting for me. Calling, even. Trying to get me back. I pictured it like a coyote howling at the moon. That lonely calling.

Then I remembered I didn't have to tell anybody anything, ever again. There would be no Pat. No program. No working on myself or trying to get fixed. I never had to do that again, and it was such a relief. It's like I'd been holding my stomach in for months, worrying about the way I looked, and I finally got to let go and relax.

Before I even had time to enjoy that feeling of letting go, I heard somebody climbing up the ladder steps of my tree. A head came up through the hole in the floor. I couldn't see who it was. I wasn't sure I cared. So long as it wasn't Zack.

"Can I come up?" Pat. I knew from the voice.

"I don't know. Can you?" I guess I was being cruel. I wasn't sure she could fit. She did. Just my luck. "What are you doing here, Pat?" When I heard my voice, I knew I was drunker than I thought. I could hear the words all kind of mush together. I tried real hard to keep them sorted out but they had a life of their own.

She sat down on the mattress beside me. "Zack called me."

I opened my mouth to say something and started to cry. It came on so sudden it scared me. I always try not to really get going when I cry. Maybe I'll never be able to stop. She put an arm around my shoulder and held on real tight. I wanted to push her away, get her off me, but I didn't have the energy.

"So, you were right," I said. "Are you happy?"

"Of course I'm not happy. You think I wanted to see you get hurt? Thing is, the way you were going, it was going to be bad no matter how it turned out. Either way, you were gonna get hurt. That's the only reason I tried to warn you."

"Okay, I'm an idiot. I get that now."

Pat made a little clucking noise with her tongue. Pulled me in even closer and sort of rocked me a little. At first I felt like she was going to smother me. Then after a while that seemed okay. I'd sink down into Pat and stop breathing. Maybe she would even breathe for me. I didn't know. Or care.

"Honey," she said, "there's nothing wrong with loving somebody."

"You acted like there was."

"It's okay that you love Zack. That's normal. If he'd taken advantage, that's what would've been the bad thing. But he was too good for that. He wouldn't do that to you. So, you see? You picked a good person to love. Trick is, next time, pick someone who's a good person and also somebody you could actually be with. You'll get better at it. Nobody really has an easy time with love. Especially us. It takes us a lot of practice."

I almost wanted to ask her what "us" meant. But I knew. Pat was one of the broken ones. Like me. It hit me, just like that. I just didn't recognize it in her at first, because she'd stopped acting so messed up, long before we ever met. Suddenly I could see her as a fourteen-year-old girl, being miserable and getting in trouble and having to go to AA and getting her heart broken. When she said she was like me, that's what she meant. Not like she was now. Like what she could still remember.

I put my arms around her as best I could and got to crying so hard I thought I'd never come up out of it again. I think I was getting her shirt all nasty and wet but she didn't seem to mind and I couldn't have stopped if I'd tried.

136

Then I said something I never thought I'd say out loud to anybody. Because I hadn't really even said it out loud to myself. "Bill could've died."

She was quiet for a minute. It seemed like a long minute. "Yeah, he could have. Just luck that he didn't."

"It would have been my fault. I could have killed him."

We sat there for a while, and my sniffles and hitches seemed to echo around inside the walls of Snake's blanket tent. After a bit she said, "We'll do a fourth step inventory down the road. We'll work on it together."

"I'm not going to be in the program anymore, Pat. I don't need it. Don't you get that? I'm not even an alcoholic. It's my mom who needs it. Why doesn't *she* go?"

Pat rocked me back and forth a little more. She said, "This program isn't for people who need it, honey, it's for people who want it. Most of the people who need to get sober never will. You have to want that for yourself."

I still figured I didn't want anything except to disappear.

"Mom's drinking is, like, a million times worse than mine."

"That's probably true."

"My drinking is, like . . . normal."

She was quiet for a long time. The kind of quiet that makes you worry what someone's thinking. What's about to come next. "Cynnie . . ."

"What?"

"Normal for a thirteen- or fourteen-year-old is *none*."

"Oh, come on."

"I'm telling you, girl. For a kid your age to drink . . . every

137

day . . . enough to get drunk every time . . . That's not even *close* to normal, honey. You've completely lost track of what normal is. Or maybe you never even got a chance to know."

My crying had kind of used itself up. I felt all scraped out inside. She helped me lie down, and she put her coat over me. I didn't even try to think about what she'd just said. I just tried to get some sleep.

When I woke up in the morning I found out she'd sat there with me all night, without her coat on, to make sure I'd be okay.

I tried to lift up my head. My brain felt like it had been sandpapered inside. My stomach was all full of gravel. I asked her if I could be alone. She asked if I was going to the Sunday morning meeting, but I said I was too sick.

Just as she was climbing down the ladder steps, just before her head disappeared, she said one more thing. She said, "Cynnie, did you ever stop to think that when your mother was your age, maybe she drank just about like you do now?"

After she left I climbed down and started throwing up. Even after my stomach was empty, I couldn't stop. That last thing Pat said—no matter how much I threw up, I couldn't get it out of me.

I limped into the Sunday morning meeting with sunglasses on. The world was too bright and too loud. I'd probably have to go back to the doctor for my leg, maybe even wear a cast again. I knew my mom would be mad.

I could feel Pat's eyes follow me. I looked up at her and she smiled. I sat down, very gently. I couldn't even look at the cookies. The meeting secretary, Tom, started the usual way. He asked if there was anybody with less than thirty days sober, anybody new who wanted a welcome chip.

I raised my hand. "My name is Cynthia. I'm an alcoholic."

Everybody said, "Hi, Cynthia. Welcome back." Nobody seemed surprised except me.

CHAPTER 10

After Six Months, Daylight

What can I say about my first six months? It's hard. Because Pat was right. I didn't feel much. For half a year I stumbled around like one of the undead in those bad horror flicks. It took actual contact with actual people to wake me up. So the ninth step, where I had to go around making amends to people, was a major wake-up call.

Pat waited in the car while I walked up to Harvey's new house. Well, it wasn't a house, exactly. It was more of a trailer. I could feel the knife in my pocket, that hard lumpy way it pushed on my leg, like on the day I took it. I tried to remind myself that I wasn't quite the same person anymore. I could hear my heart pounding in my ears.

Harvey's trailer had cinder-block steps that I had to stand on to reach the door. I knocked. On about the count of three I figured he must not be home, so I felt a lot better. Then he opened the door.

His face changed to see me. His eyes got all suspicious and he took a step back, like the only thing I could possibly bring to his door was trouble. At first I wanted to be mad about that. Like, it was so typical of Harvey to think the worst about me. Then I reminded myself that the worst had pretty much turned out to be true about me. At least with the knife.

Pat says that's why you have to do this. So you can see in people's eyes how you really were. Then you have to admit how bad things had gotten. She said it doesn't matter much if they forgive you or if they don't. Just so long as you know you did your best to make it right.

"What the hell do *you* want?" he said. He had this look on his face like he'd just smelled something spoiled. I held the knife out on the open palm of my hand. We both just looked at it for a minute. Then he said, "I suppose now you're gonna tell me you found it layin' around."

"No, sir. I stole it." I held it further out to him and he took it off my hand.

"How come you're bringin' it back now?"

"Because it's yours. Because I was wrong to take it."

He didn't look quite convinced yet. He looked braced for a bad surprise, maybe some kind of trick. "You got a conscience? Is that it?"

I had to think about that for a minute. I said, "I'm pretty

sure everybody does, in there somewhere. I'm trying to find mine." Pat says if you want to be honest, you start by acting honest. After a while the real thing sort of catches up with you.

I think that was more of an honest answer than he expected. He looked at me for a long time, real hard, like if he looked hard enough he might see what he wanted to know. Then he said, "My granddad gave me this knife. That's why I was so mad."

I nodded, even though I hadn't known that. I hadn't known it was important to him. I thought he had lots of things and this was just one more. "I'm sorry I stole from you."

He shrugged his shoulders. He didn't seem to want to dislike me anymore. Not that he liked me or anything. Just that it wasn't so important to be mad. Maybe it was too much trouble all of a sudden. "Well, it's back now," he said. "That's the main thing."

He closed the door without saying goodbye, and I walked back to Pat's car.

"That was a hard one to do, huh?" she said.

"Nah. Not so bad. Not like the last one. Not like the next ones."

"Who's left on your list?"

"My mom. And Snake, except he's gone. And Bill."

"And Zack."

"No way, Pat. I don't owe Zack an apology. I don't owe him anything. Not after what he said to me. Besides, I didn't do anything to him. You said yourself there's nothing wrong with loving somebody."

"That's not the part I think you should apologize for. It's

142

the part where you been treating him like poison just because he did something you didn't like, even though he didn't do anything wrong. Want to know why you're so furious over what he said?"

"No."

"Tell you anyway. 'Cause of the grain of truth to it. Somebody says something to you and it's just not true, you'd never take it so hard. But that one thing we mean to deny, when somebody else points it out . . . man, we just hit the ceiling. Just about everybody I ever met said some kind of vow that they'd never grow up like their mother. Or father. And then somewhere down the line it hits you—you did anyway, in spite of all your trying. It's one of life's little mean tricks."

"So you're telling me I'm going to turn out like my mom, period, and there's nothing I can do about it."

"No, but I *am* saying you can't avoid it by trying to control it with your own willpower. You have to really heal all that old crap that runs in the family."

"Let me get this straight. What you're saying to me is exactly what Zack said to me. You're agreeing with him."

Pat sighed. "There's a saying in the program. 'The truth shall set you free—' "

Big deal, I thought, there's that same stale old saying everywhere.

" '—but first it shall piss you off.' "

I laughed. I didn't mean to. It was this little pig snort that leaked out of me against my will. I hated it when Pat made me laugh when I was trying to stay mad.

"I'm not making amends to Zack."

"Oh, I expect you will," she said. "If I stay out of your way and give you some time."

She started up the car and we drove in silence for a while. I was thinking about a thing she said once, how you're only as sick as your secrets.

I said, "There's something I left off when we did my inventory." She just waited. "That night you came up to my tree house. I had that pocketknife out. And open. I was thinking about using it. You know. On myself."

"How serious do you think you were?"

"I don't know." I wasn't trying to duck the question. It was true. I didn't know.

She was quiet for a minute, but I could see her chewing on that one. I could almost see it going around in her brain. "Well," she said, "I guess you'll have to make some amends to yourself while you're at it."

"Now how the hell am I supposed to make amends to myself?"

"Don't hurt yourself anymore."

It was like someone opened up the curtains and let light into the room, and all of a sudden I could see it was daylight, and had been all this time.

That night, after my mom got drunk, she slammed open the door to my room and started yelling at me. I was asleep, so it took me a minute to figure out what was going on.

A lot of what she said didn't make sense, but I heard her say that *she* shouldn't have to get sober just because *I* was on the program. She was really upset. It scared me.

144

"I never said you should." I'd thought it, though.

"No, but I can tell. You think just because you can do it, I should do it, too."

"I didn't say that!"

"Hah!" she screamed, and slammed the door.

I lay awake for hours listening to her pop one beer can after another. Hoping she would pass out and not come in screaming again. I had no idea what brought that on.

I was sharing in a meeting. In fact, I was sharing first, leading, because it was a birthday for me. Sort of. Well, a half birthday. It was my six months. And nobody else was taking a chip, so unfortunately the focus was on me.

I was talking about how my sponsor had me working on step eight and nine. Going around making amends to people. I said, "Only, one of the people I really want to make amends to, I'm not sure where he is." I meant Snake, but I thought it'd be better not to name names.

Pat nudged me in the ribs. I'd been looking down at the table, because it was still kind of embarrassing to share. Even after all the practice. I looked up. I saw my mom walk in and sit down. I could feel my face get red. I didn't say a word for a minute. But it was still my turn to share, until I passed it on to somebody, so nobody else said anything, either. I kept staring at my mom. I couldn't figure out if she was here for me, like to tell me something, or if she was here for her. She wasn't looking at me. She was looking at Zack. I bet she was thinking she didn't want to share with him there. I knew how she felt. I didn't want to talk in front of *her*. But everybody was waiting for me to go on.

145

"One of my amends went kind of bad," I said. "I guess that happens to everybody. This kid I used to know. I sort of . . . well, I broke his nose, actually. Because he said something about—" I looked at my mom again. She was watching me and listening now, like I was a stranger, someone she might learn something from. "—well, about, you know, somebody I thought I oughta stand up for. Anyway, I apologized. But he pretty much told me to go to hell. Not quite that polite." Everybody laughed. I couldn't go on. I just couldn't. I could not talk with my mom sitting there staring at me. So I just said, "I guess that's all for now."

I called on Zack. I missed most of what he said, trying not to look at my mom.

After the meeting she slipped out. She didn't stay for the part at the end, where we stand in a circle and say the Serenity Prayer. She sort of spun away without any noise about it. I thought maybe I'd dreamed the whole thing up.

Zack came up to me and said, "Hi, Cynthia." Nobody called me Cynnie now. I never even had to ask them not to. They just sort of saw on their own that I had grown up some. But until Zack said it just then, I didn't know what he called me anymore. Because we hadn't talked for a long time. Zack said, "I had something like that happen to me."

I thought he meant his mom showed up at a meeting. I had my mom on the brain. Also, I was upset because he was talking to me. I couldn't look at his face so I looked at the floor. My throat felt weird inside. "Oh yeah?"

"Yeah, I went back to this guy I used to work for. Told him I lifted a few dollars out of the till. I said I'd pay it back when I could. He said, 'Admitting you're a thief doesn't make you any less a thief.' "

"Oh. Like Richie, you mean. What'd you say?"

"I said, 'Well, maybe so, but I'm not going to steal anymore, and *that* makes me a *lot* less of a thief.' He never did cut me any slack, though. Even when I paid him back. Hey. You got a minute to talk?"

"Yeah. Sure."

I heard myself say it to him like I was listening to somebody else. I could've sworn I was about to tell him to go to hell. But then somebody with my voice said "okay." And all I could do was watch it, like I was in some other part of the room. Like I wasn't even in my body.

We sat in a couple of chairs at the very back.

"I wanted to make an amends to you," he said. Right away I felt like I wanted to cry, but I didn't let that happen. "I handled things so wrong with you and me. I'm so sorry. I *do* like you. I always did. Just not like that. But I didn't know what to say to you or what to do and I ended up making a big mess of things, and I know I really hurt you with what I said. I should've said something sooner. And I'm sorry for that. Really sorry. But what I'm most sorry for is sort of . . . I don't know how to say it." A long pause. "The loneliest I ever was in my life is when I was with Rita. I shouldn't have used you to try to fix it. I'm not just saying it because I need to say it to get through a step. I really feel bad about it."

147

I still couldn't look at his face.

"Yeah. Okay."

"So . . . you forgive me?"

"Sure."

But we could both hear by the way I said it that even if I was trying to forgive him, I wasn't doing such a great job.

Just before we walked out the door together he said, "What was your mom doing here? Is she in the program now?"

So. I hadn't dreamed the whole thing up.

"Zack," I said, "your guess is just about as good as mine."

Pat was waiting for me outside.

"I'm real proud of you," she said.

"For what?" Now I had Zack on the brain. I thought maybe she was proud of me for sitting down and talking to him, or maybe she even thought I was back there making my amends.

"For your six months, what do you think?"

"Oh. Right."

"I know that thing with your mother threw you."

"You have no idea."

"Anyway. Got a present for you."

"You do?"

She looked at me sideways and laughed because of the way I said it. I guess I made it sound like she'd just said I won seventy million dollars or something. "Didn't anybody ever give you a present before?"

We started walking together, toward her car. "Not lately," I said. "And even when my mom used to get me stuff, it was bad stuff. She'd get me dresses. I hate dresses. But she wanted me to like them. So she'd get me dresses. Which is even worse than most lame presents, because it wasn't even really a present. I mean, it wasn't for me. It was for her. I always really resented that."

We got to her car and got inside, and she threw this little envelope into my lap. It didn't look like a present. It just looked like a card.

"It's not a dress," she said.

I picked it up and shook it, just to be funny. Just to be a punk. "You sure?" Something slid around in there.

I opened it up, and inside was a phone card. A prepaid phone card.

"Oh, my God," I said. First I couldn't talk at all. Then, after a bit, I said, "This is the best present ever."

"It's not *that* big of a deal," she said. Like I was embarrassing her.

"Yes, it is. It totally is." It was the first time someone gave me something that showed they were actually listening. That they actually listened to me, to hear what I would want. "It *is* a big deal," I said. "Because it's actually for me."

A minute later, while we were driving, I said, "Remember when you said that thing to me about not being able to feel my feelings? You said people will say something bores them, and they don't even know they're really scared? I was scared to death to get a job. Or even look for one. I didn't know it until just now, when I could feel how relieved I was that I didn't have to."

"Everybody's scared of stuff like that," she said.

"Really?"

"Especially when they're feeling vulnerable for some reason."

"Yeah. I felt like, maybe later, when I sort of . . . have my feet on the ground more. But my life feels so . . . overwhelming. I just couldn't add on something scary like that."

"Does this make you feel any more sympathetic toward your mom?"

At first I didn't even get what she meant, and I guess it showed.

"Didn't you jump all over your mom because she won't go out and get a job?"

"Well, yeah, but . . . she's the mom. She really should."

"Okay, granted. But now do you get why it's hard?"

I knew I should. I heard what she was saying. But I wasn't quite feeling it.

"I'll work on it," I said.

When I got home, my mom was in the kitchen, standing at the sink, pouring a big quart bottle of gin down the drain. She turned when she saw me come in. We looked at each other's faces for a minute. I don't think she was drunk.

I said, "So. You're serious about this."

She smiled in that way that didn't make her look happy. "I guess I can do it if you can."

I nodded, but I didn't say anything. I wasn't so sure about this. Those meetings felt kind of private. My new place. I wasn't sure I wanted to share all that with my mom. But it felt like one of those thoughts you're not supposed to have. I figured I'd talk to Pat about it. I could talk to Pat about anything. Even weird stuff like that.

She went into the living room and sat down on the very edge of the couch, kind of perched there, like the couch was the wrong size all of a sudden. She looked uncomfortable.

She hadn't thrown the bottle away; it was just sitting there on the counter. Even though it was empty, it made me a little nervous. So I stuffed it way down in the kitchen trash. When I looked up she was sitting the same weird way, but with her fingers all laced together in her lap, like she had no idea what to do with them. She looked up and saw me watching her.

"What am I supposed to do all day, Cynthia?"

I remembered how that felt.

I went in my room and got my Big Book. That's what they call the book about AA. It's sort of like a textbook. I brought it out and set it in her lap.

"Here," I said. "Do some reading. It passes the time."

When I called Pat that night, like I did every night, we didn't really talk all that much about what happened with my mom. I mean, what was there really to say? We both knew it made me uncomfortable. But I had to at least try to be supportive. Besides, I didn't figure it would last. That's a horrible thing to say, I know. But it's the God's honest truth.

We talked more about Zack.

"Do I have to forgive him for what he said to me? Just because he wants me to?"

Pat said, "That's actually a two-part question. You definitely don't have to do it because he wants you to. You're doing it for you. And you don't have to, no. But it really makes us sick when we hang on to resentments like that."

"Why *should* I forgive him? Maybe that's a better question."

"Well, let me see. How much time do you have? How 'bout because he said it out of caring for you? He saw you were on the wrong road, and he was trying to warn you. And ever since then you been on a better path. You might never have gotten sober and straightened around for real if he hadn't been there with that wake-up call. How 'bout the fact that it hurts you a lot more than it hurts him when you don't? You're hanging on to all this hurt and anger, and who is it hurting? You or him? It's like you're so mad at him, you're beating yourself up. It doesn't make good sense."

I sighed. I sort of got what she meant. But I didn't feel any more ready to do it.

"Give it a little more time," she said. "Work on another one in the meantime. An easier one. Like that boy with the weird nickname."

"Snake's gone, though."

"You can still do the work. Write down the amends. And then just put it aside. If you ever see him again, you'll give it to him. That's all you can do for now. Except you might say a little prayer that shows you're *willing* to make your amends to him. You know. If you ever got the chance. So long as you're willing. That's the most important part of the whole deal, right there."

I sat up in my tree house having more thoughts I probably shouldn't have had. I was thinking, Now every time I go in the house she'll want to . . . like . . . talk to me. Or something. I'd gotten used to sort of living on my own almost. I wasn't sure how much I wanted to get to know her.

I knew I should've told more of this stuff to Pat.

Then I said a little prayer about Snake. I guess you could call it a prayer. I wasn't too sure about the whole God thing, but Pat said you don't have to call your Higher Power "God" if you don't want. She said at first use the group. A whole group of people trying to get healthy is bigger and more powerful than one little member, right? But I couldn't exactly pray to my AA group. So I just sort of said prayers and threw them out there, like when you put a message in a bottle and throw it in the ocean, and you don't know yet who's going to get it. Maybe I'd get clearer on that stuff later on.

I said I was sorry about what happened with Snake, and that I didn't know where he was, but if I did, I'd tell him. I'd try to make it right with him. I said, whoever you are out there, just so you know, if you want me to make amends to Snake, walk him by here. I'll do my bit.

I stayed up there all afternoon and evening, writing letters to Snake even though I wouldn't know where to send them. I wrote about ten. Each one seemed to get a little closer to the right things to say.

Somewhere around bedtime my mom came out and stood under the tree and called up and asked if we had any milk.

That seemed like a weird question. I mean, did she forget where we keep it, or what?

"I dunno," I said. "Look in the fridge."

"I did. There's none in there."

"Well, where the hell else would it be?" I could hear my voice go up as I said it. I was trying not to be snotty to my mom, but this was just too much. "I mean, you just open the refrigerator door. It's either there or it's not. This is not brain surgery. Milk is in the fridge."

Then everything just got quiet, and I got to feel bad for what I said. Just like the old days. I looked down and she was looking at the ground. Hurt.

That's when it hit me that she'd been asking me to help. I closed my eyes and sighed. "Want me to run to the store and get some?"

"Would you, Cynthia? That would be nice. I thought some hot milk might help me sleep."

I climbed down and she gave me a couple of dollars and I ran to the market.

On the way back, there was this guy, this kid, walking behind me. First on the other side of the street. Then on my side. I was starting to get nervous. He was getting a little closer. I was just about to break into a run.

I heard him say, "Hey! Cynnie!"

I stopped and turned around.

It hardly looked like Snake at all. His hair was all grown out, and he didn't look chunky. He looked older. But I knew it was him. I guess I partway knew it would be.

I was kind of expecting him.

⁘ ⁘ ⁘

Snake snuck up into my tree house while I brought the milk in to my mom. I tried to slip in and out real quietly, but she heard me.

"Know what I was thinking, Cynthia?"

Oh, God, I thought. Not now. Please not now. I wanted to get up into the tree house and talk to Snake. See where he'd been. If he was staying. If he was mad at me or what. Please just let me slip out again.

But she stuck her head in the kitchen and went on. "I was thinking maybe we could get Bill back here for the summer."

I dropped the milk carton on the floor. But that just dented it. I didn't lose any of the milk or anything. "Are you serious?"

"Well, yeah. I was just thinking, if I'm sober, and you're home from school, we oughta be able to take care of him. Right? Between the two of us?"

"Of course we can. I'll do all the work." I always did, I almost said, but I caught myself. This was no time to be snotty. "God, that would be so great!"

"I know how much you miss him," she said.

Then she disappeared, and I stood there, leaning on the sink, thinking about that last thing she said. I guess I always thought she didn't get that. How much I missed him. And now that I knew she did, had all along, I couldn't figure out which was worse: if she knew and didn't fix it, or if she didn't get it at all. But she was offering to fix it the best she could. For a whole summer! But then I started thinking how awful it would be to say goodbye all over again in the fall. But that still

155

had to be better than not seeing him at all. Then I thought how she said *I* missed him, but she didn't say if *she* did.

I went into my room and lay on my back on the bed, and stared at the ceiling, and tried to let it all in. Just let all that different stuff roll around in my head.

I'm guessing that went on for a good five or ten minutes before it hit me what I'd forgotten.

I was on the cot mattress, and Snake was lying on the tree house floor. We both had our hands laced behind our heads, and we were looking up through the leaves at the stars. I think my mom was downstairs drinking warm milk, but I couldn't be sure. Even when I wasn't looking at him, it didn't feel the same to be with him. *He* didn't feel the same. And I guess neither did I.

He said, "Maybe we shoulda put more like a top on this, huh? I just ran out of blankets."

"Nah. I like it like this. I wouldn't want to keep the stars out."

"Remember when we were building this?"

"Yeah," I said. "Only it seems like a real long time ago now. Like a former lifetime or something. Where were you?"

"Kind of all around. I hitched a ride on this flatbed truck with a bunch of guys who were doing stuff they call 'casual labor.' Picking crops, mostly. It's pretty good work. Nobody cares who the hell you are. They just point and you work and at the end of the day they pay cash. I think I was back in California most of the time."

I thought about the letters I'd been writing him all day. I wished it was light so I could tell which was which. The last one was the best. If I knew which it was, I'd have given it to him right then.

I said, "You're really brave."

"No, I'm not. I was scared the whole time."

"But you did it, though."

He didn't say anything for a long time. I could hear him breathing. "If I was brave, I'd have gone home. I didn't want to get hit in the face anymore. I kind of lost the stomach for it."

"Why'd you come back?"

"I don't know. It's weird not being home wherever you go. It's like you're always somewhere, but it never feels quite right."

"Did you see your dad yet?"

"No. And I'm not going to, either."

"Where are you gonna stay?"

He didn't answer, and I didn't ask any more questions. We looked at the stars for a while, the way the dark shapes of the leaves shifted around in between. I was thinking that he used to be my boyfriend but back then I didn't much want him to be. Now I wondered why I'd been so sure back then. I wasn't sure how I felt about that whole deal now.

After a while I went downstairs and called Pat. It was so weird and amazing, what had just happened. I couldn't wait to tell her.

I said, "Pat. The weirdest thing happened. You're not

going to believe it. I just said this prayer that if I saw Snake, I'd make amends to him. And guess what?"

Pat said, "Let me guess. You bumped into him about a second later."

I was so excited about the whole thing, I forgot to ask how she knew. I just said, "Yeah. Weird, huh?"

Pat said, "I don't think I'd call it weird, no."

"Well, what would you call it, then? If it's not weird?"

It was quiet on the line for a second, like she was waiting for me to think of it myself. Then she said, "I'd call it your Higher Power working in your life. I wish I had a nickel for every time I heard a story just like that."

I didn't even answer. At first it made me kind of mad. I told her about this wonderful, amazing thing, this miracle, and she was acting like it was no big deal. Like it was just the normal way of things. But then I thought, maybe it would be cool to be like Pat and live in a world where miracles were just the normal everyday thing.

Pat said, "You made your amends yet?"

"Not yet. I wrote stuff out for him. But I didn't give it to him yet."

"Well, go on," she said, and we got off the phone.

As soon as we did, I realized I hadn't even told her about Bill. It felt like there was too much happening at once. Good stuff, pretty much. Just too much of it.

I made Snake a baloney and cheese sandwich and a glass of milk. I was glad we had milk. I'd brought that big pile of letters downstairs with me, and I dug around until I found the best one, and I put it on the plate with the sandwich. I took the milk up first, but it turned out Snake was already asleep. I knew he must have been real tired. I went back for the sandwich and the letter. I left the whole thing beside the mattress, for morning.

I slept in my room downstairs. Just before I fell asleep I thought, That worked out pretty good for something I didn't even understand. I thought, Maybe I'm not even supposed to understand. Maybe if I put a message in a bottle for God, maybe only God needs to know how it gets where it's going. Maybe that was never my job at all.

Then I went back to thinking about Bill.

CHAPTER 11

A Girl Needs a Momma

The meeting started at five. My mom showed up. I hadn't had time to talk to Pat much about that. There'd been too much going on.

When I got called on to share, I just talked about amends in general, and about forgiveness. I didn't say anything about Snake. About the little note he left for me in the tree house. I had it in my pocket, but I thought it might be better to talk to Pat about that privately. Especially with my mom hanging around.

Once while I was sharing I looked at Zack and he was looking right at me, and he looked really sad. It felt awful to see him looking so sad. I felt so bad about it, I almost didn't have room to feel mad anymore.

When I was done sharing I could tell my mom wanted to talk. She was leaning forward, staring at me, and her eyes said, Pick me. Pick me. But I wasn't sure how. Was I supposed to call her "Mom" in front of all these people? Or "Rita"? It seemed rude to point like you do with a stranger. I said, "Does anybody *feel* like sharing?"

She raised her hand. I wanted to tell her you don't have to do that. Just say your name and start. I nodded at her. More than ever, I was wishing she wasn't here.

"My name is Rita," she said. "I'm an alcoholic." It felt weird to hear her admit it.

"I haven't been sober for what you'd call a long time. Just about—" She looked at her watch. "—maybe thirty-six hours." She got a round of applause. That surprised her. In AA people always applaud the time you've got. No matter how short it is. They know it's a long time to the person who just got it.

I was hoping she wouldn't say much more, but she did.

"It wasn't always this bad. The drinking, I mean. Used to be something I could control pretty good before Cynthia's father died. That's when everything just sorta went to hell. I'd gotten pregnant with my first girl when I was just a kid, just a couple years older than Cynthia. The guy took off and I was on my own all those years. And then I met Billy. He was just such a wonderful guy. He adopted my oldest girl. How many guys would do that? And then we had Cynthia, and our lives was going along so good until he got killed in that boiler explosion at his work. There I was with this thirteen-year-old girl, just getting rebellious, and this clingy three-year-old girl. She needed me and she needed her daddy and I had to work

161

and I couldn't be all those things, and all the time thinking Billy was the only real true love in my whole life and now here he was already gone. I just missed him so much."

She started to cry. I could hear it in her voice. I was looking down, running my fingernail along the plastic molding on the edge of the table.

I got this terrible feeling all over, and then a minute later I knew why. Those three silver dollars. I hadn't thought about that at all. It's like I made myself forget. It made me feel like the worst person on the whole planet. How can you make amends to a person who's already dead? Or maybe the person I should be sorry to was me. I would never have those dollars again. I couldn't believe I did that to myself. For a crappy bottle of wine.

I tried to think what I could remember about my dad. I remember he used to carry me on his shoulders, with my arms around his forehead, holding on, and he'd hold my ankles. Sometimes my hands would slip down over his eyes and he'd grope around like a blind man and say, "Who shut off the lights?" And I'd laugh. I thought I remembered how he'd take me sometimes to his favorite pub and sit me up on the bar, and I got to have either a pickled egg or a pickled pig's foot, and I always took the pig's foot because it was bigger. But maybe I just remember being told about that. Maybe it never happened. Now I wouldn't eat a pickled pig's foot on a bet, but I was only three.

It was real hard to hear my mom cry.

"No matter what I do," she said, "I don't think that girl

ever can forgive me, and I don't guess I blame her. Running this long string of men through the house in front of her, and her having to raise herself up, and her brother Bill in the deal. Girl needs a momma. Sometimes I dream about Billy at night and I tell him I'm sorry I did such a lousy job with his daughter. I only had all those boyfriends trying to find a man like the one I lost. I know you got to make amends down the line, but I just can't figure how I'll ever make it right with my kids. Poor little Bill. Sometimes when I can't sleep at night I get to thinking maybe if I hadn't kept drinking while I was pregnant with him—" Her voice kind of broke off with a crack, like a dry stick snapping. Then she got real quiet. "Maybe he wouldn't have the problems he's got."

My face and my stomach got all tingly. I had never once thought about that.

By now she was crying hard enough that she couldn't keep going. She just sort of waved her hand to pass it on to somebody else. The somebody else was Phyllis, the new secretary.

Phyllis reached over and patted my mom's hand. She said, "Rita, honey, just keep coming back to these meetings. Not a one of us can undo everything we did. Can't change the past, but there's always the future. Just keep coming back."

Then Phyllis went on sharing about her own stuff, and Pat reached over and squeezed my arm a little. People I knew in the meeting looked at me and smiled. I was right on the edge of crying. I guess it showed.

After the meeting my mom went home by herself. Pat and I stayed after. We were on the clean-up committee. We were in the big utility kitchen and Pat had one of those giant coffee urns upside down in the sink, washing it.

"Care to talk about it?"

I said, "You know, at first I didn't want her here at all. I didn't even like her anymore. It's like I didn't even *want* to like her. But now, you know . . . after today . . ."

She nodded, her head bobbing up and down for a few long seconds. "More you know about somebody, harder it is to stay mad."

I almost said I was never mad, I just sort of didn't care. But I didn't say it, because I started to know that it probably wasn't true. I was probably plenty mad without really knowing. And I probably did care. It takes me a long time, sometimes, to figure out how something is supposed to feel.

My mom was right about one thing. A girl does need a momma. I wasn't sure how to say that to Pat. Like, all of a sudden, for the first time ever, I was thinking, Maybe she really *will* get sober. And be like a mom again. And then I could be like a kid. Which would be this huge weight off me. I wondered if this was how my dad felt, having to lug me on his shoulders with my hands over his eyes. You can get used to a weight like that and almost forget you've got it. But it sure would feel good to put it down.

I said to Pat, "You know, if she really does stay sober, we're going to get Bill back for the summer."

She said, "Well. If she does. Give it some time."

"Maybe after a while we could get him back for good. We could be like a real family."

"Don't jump too far down the road."

"You think she won't do it?"

"I didn't say that."

"Why can't you just believe in this?" I was getting mad now. I could feel it. We could both hear it on me.

She rinsed soap out of both those big urns and set them to drip in the sink. She dried her hands off on a paper towel. I had my hands on my hips, waiting for an answer.

"Honey, I can't even tell you for a fact that *I'll* be sober tomorrow. Remember, it's one day at a time." I thought that was a bad answer, but I didn't say so. "It's just that I see a lot of people come and go in this program. I hope she makes it. Maybe she will. Just wait a while to see."

I ran into Zack outside. I don't think he was waiting for me. He was talking to that guy Earl. But it felt weird that I needed him to be there and then he was, kind of like the thing with Snake.

He looked up at me, and then Earl said "so long" and then it was just the two of us.

I said, "Hey, Zack."

He said, "Hey." Then he said, "I know you don't really forgive me. But it's okay. It was a terrible thing to say."

"Yeah, but it helped get me straightened around. And you called Pat. So I know you must've cared about me. Plus you cared enough to tell me the truth. Even if I hated it. I didn't handle things so great, either. I'm sorry I've been treating you like poison when all you did was try to do the right thing."

Nobody said anything for a minute. So I looked up. He had his hand stuck out to me, like he was waiting for me to shake it. So I did.

"Friends?" he asked.

"Yeah," I said. Actually, I was thinking, Maybe eventually. Maybe we'll be friends again eventually, and at least in the meantime we can look at each other. But I didn't say that. I left well enough alone.

The whole next day in school I carried around the note Snake had left for me in the tree house. I could feel it in my pocket. I took it out and read it again during Mr. Werther's art class.

It was written on the torn-off end of the last page of my letter, the blank space at the end where I ran out of stuff to say. I guess he took the rest with him, like something he'd want to keep.

It said, "Cynnie, thanks for this. And thanks for the food."

Trouble was, he didn't say where he was or when he was coming back. Or what he actually thought about what I said in my letter. I guess that's why I couldn't get it off my mind. Just as I folded it up and put it back in my pocket, Mr. Werther slipped by behind my shoulder. We were supposed to be sketching quietly on our own. I wasn't doing anything artistic when he came by.

He said, "See me after class, okay?"

My stomach got this heavy feel like somebody dropped

something into it from a long way up. I thought, I'll just never be able to win with this guy. He's got it out for me now, and nothing I do will ever be good enough.

When the bell rang I just sat there waiting. At least I had a meeting to go to after school. That always helps a little. Pat says when you share bad things in a meeting, you get to leave half behind, plus you get the courage to hold up the other half. He walked down the aisle.

I said, "I wasn't passing notes, Mr. Werther. I was just reading a note somebody left me. Days ago. Not even in school. But I know, I was supposed to be drawing. I'm sorry. I just couldn't stop thinking about that note."

He sat on the edge of the desk across the aisle. He didn't look mad. "I didn't see any note."

"Oh. Me and my big mouth, then, huh?" We both smiled for a minute. "So, why am I here, then?"

"I just want to say how nice it is to see you get better."

I was so surprised I couldn't think what to say at first. Then I said, "How can you see that?"

"It's all over your face. I can see it in your eyes. You look like you grew up about four years' worth since you left. We were worried about you, you know."

"Who's we?" I knew he couldn't be talking about other kids. The other kids in this school would be real surprised to discover I'd been born in the first place.

"Your teachers. The principal. We're just glad things seem to be getting better for you."

I got up to go, because it was embarrassing, having

somebody act like they care like that. Kind of nice, but embarrassing. I said, "Yeah, a little better. At least I remembered you told me to stay after class."

He laughed. "Well, keep up the good work, Cynthia."

Good work. Nobody ever gave me credit for good work before. I wondered if this was the first time I'd ever done any.

Just as I was walking out the door he said, "I'm tempted to ask you again. About art club."

I stopped. Looked back over my shoulder at him. "Art club?" I was trying to think if I had ever talked about it with him before.

"I asked you twice last year, but you pretty much blew me off."

"Yeah," I said. "Sorry. Last year I pretty much blew everything off."

"You do remember my asking, though. Right?"

That was something like being busted. That was when I knew he could just look at my face and see that I barely remembered talking about it. I had some sort of little sketchy memory. I mean, at least it sounded familiar. But—I don't know how to explain this—it's like it never really went all the way into my ears before. I guess the idea of staying at school longer than I had to was just so foreign to me. I must've heard it like he'd been speaking some other language.

"Um, yeah," I said. It didn't sound too convincing. "Pretty much."

"Well, it's Wednesday and Friday, if you change your mind."

I think at that point I was still pretty sure I wouldn't. But then just as I left his room and swung around the corner into the hall, I got curious about something. And it was so important, I actually went back. And I didn't even know *why* it was so important. But it was.

I leaned my shoulder on his door frame, but he didn't see me or look up. He was reading something on his desk.

"Mr. Werther?" He looked up. Surprised. I could see he'd expected me to run and keep running. Like always. "Do you invite all your students to join art club?"

He looked into my face for a second. I felt like he knew why this was an important question. Which is weird, because I still didn't. "No. Just the ones I think have talent."

I think I just stood there nodding for a minute. Then I couldn't think what else to do, so I went home.

When I got home, before I could even get in the door, I heard a little hissing sound. I looked up to the tree house and there was Snake, looking down at me through the hole in the blanket. I climbed up and we sat awhile.

"Where'd you go today?" I asked.

"Had to go out and look for work. I'm gonna be at Uncle Ted's junkyard awhile. There's a couch in the office. He said he won't tell my dad where I'm staying. Why are you looking at me like that?"

"Like what?" It was the first time I'd seen him in daylight since he got back. I couldn't get over how much he'd changed. His face was thinner. He had muscles in his arms. His hair was the color of the reddish-blond wood on our dining room table.

"I don't know, like . . . I don't know."

"So I guess you're never going back to school, huh?"

"I'll go back. When I'm sixteen. It's only a few more months. When I'm sixteen I can be an emancipated minor."

He explained to me what that was. This deal where if you can take care of yourself and earn money and have a place to live, you can just sort of call yourself an adult early. It's legal.

I said, "Are you still gonna come over?"

"You want me to?"

"Well, sure I do."

He was quiet for a minute, picking at a loose thread on the edge of the mattress. Then he said, "I just sort of finally got used to the idea that you didn't like me much."

"No, I do. It just takes me a long time, sometimes. To figure out how I feel about something. By the time I figured out I liked you, you were already gone."

That seemed to make sense to him. Not just anybody can understand a thing like that.

The next few days I drew a lot of pictures. I looked out the window and sketched the house next door. I drew my favorite tree, the one with the tree house. I drew a bunch of pictures of Bill, partly from the picture Nanny and Grampop sent me, partly from memory. I even drew my mom when she was watching TV and not paying any attention to me.

And it's funny, because all this time I was telling myself I wasn't going to art club. But if I was wrong, and I did go, part of me felt like I needed to know more about art. This was a thing of mine, and I'm not sure why I did it, but it's one of those things you just can't stop yourself from doing. The summer before I went into the first grade I made a girl from down the street teach me the alphabet. Because I figured you needed to know that for the first grade. Like it never occurred to me I was going there to learn it like everybody else.

I keep thinking I'm going to get busted somehow for not knowing the right stuff.

One of the pictures of Bill was pretty good, so I sent it to Nanny and Grampop along with a letter. It was this brainstorm I had. Because my phone card was about to run out. And I was trying to think of a way to get them to help me. And they still weren't real big fans of mine after everything that had happened.

In the letter I told them how long I'd been sober, and what it was like to work with Pat, and the kind of stuff we worked on together. I told them about Mom coming to meetings because she saw how things got better for me when I did it. I even told them about joining art club, because I thought it made me sound like I was more involved with school.

Then I asked the favor. I asked if I wrote letters to Bill two or three times a week, would they read them to him? I tried to keep it kind of light and chatty.

I was getting desperate, and I couldn't think what else to do.

Then, after I mailed the letter, I realized I really had to go to art club. Otherwise I was a liar, and if they found out, they'd never trust me again. And even if they didn't find out, I'd know I was a liar. And the only way to solve the problem I'd just made was to join.

Join. What a weird word. I'm not sure I'd ever used that word before. I mean, about me, that is.

The next day I told Mr. Werther I was going to join. I made myself say that word.

But then I blew off the next three club days.

Finally one day he just stood right in front of me as I was trying to get out of his class and made me tell him the first day I was coming.

"Okay, Friday," I said. With this little catch in my stomach where I knew I would really have to do it.

I don't know why all this was so hard for me. I don't know why all these things—things other people do without even thinking—are so damn hard for me.

I just knew I was in art club as of that second.

I showed up on Friday a little late. I'd circled the fourth floor three times before I could bring myself to go in.

Everybody was there already. Three girls, but only one I'd ever seen before. I knew her from chemistry, but the other two didn't look familiar. And a boy I sort of knew. Once I'd heard our English teacher read a poem he wrote about being a pariah. She had to tell us what that even meant. So I figured that must mean he was smart.

And Mr. Werther was there, of course, and he had his dog there with him. Right there in school. I guess he must have gone home and gotten the dog really quick after school, but I don't know because I didn't ask. But I liked that the dog was there. It gave us all something to look at, and that made things easier.

Mr. Werther came by and gave me paper and some charcoals, and I petted the dog's head. It was a red Irish setter. Pretty. Kind of hyper, but nice. His tongue kept hanging out of his mouth sideways instead of straight. It looked funny.

"What's his name?" I asked.

Mr. Werther said she was a girl and her name was Lucy Ricardo. Lucy for short. And when I laughed, he said Irish setters were kind of like the screwball redheads of the dog world.

That's when I noticed I was sitting at the same table with the girl I knew from chemistry. Rachel, I think her name was. But I didn't even remember deciding where I would sit.

Then Mr. Werther had to try to get the dog to hold still so we could draw her in charcoal. He had to sit on a stool right behind her and keep her from getting up or lying down, and when she got distracted and turned her head he had to turn it back again.

Rachel said, "This is a lot better than still life. Last week we drew a bowl of pears."

I laughed in a way that sounded a little sarcastic. "At least pears hold still."

Mr. Werther heard me and said, "Get used to drawing actual life. It moves, but your art makes it hold still."

He didn't sound mad, though.

I liked having that dog to look at and draw, so I made up

my mind to do the best art I had ever done. I guess I'd been wanting to know if Mr. Werther was right or not, ever since he said that thing about me having some talent.

So I really focused on that dog. I really looked at her and tried to see what made her look exactly the way she looked, and not like any other dog. It was a weird but kind of interesting feeling, because usually I'm all in my own head, half in the room and half out of it. But I really had to be there to look at the dog.

I decided it was the shine in her eyes and her smile. She had this big open-mouthed grin all the time. And I decided that was more important about this dog than the fact that she was red and had long hair. All Irish setters have long red hair. But this one's shiny eyes and goofy smile made her Lucy Ricardo, Mr. Werther's dog, and not any other Irish setter in the world. The others might have shiny eyes and a big smile, but not these eyes or this smile. Everybody is a little different. People, dogs. Even birds. Snowflakes, if you live somewhere they have snowflakes. No two are exactly the same.

So I didn't concentrate much on the shape of her body. I just kind of softly showed it with a few lines. But I really worked hard on the eyes and the smile.

After what felt like about ten minutes, Mr. Werther said, "Time."

I looked up at the clock and saw I'd been drawing for almost an hour and a half.

The other kids got up and gave their drawings to Mr.

Werther. The boy who wrote the poem looked over his shoulder at me. I just sat there.

Mr. Werther came by and stood in front of the table, and I could feel Lucy Ricardo sniffing at the knees of my jeans. I could feel Rachel standing there behind me, like she was waiting for me to get done so she could talk to me. I wasn't used to all this attention. It made me nervous.

Mr. Werther said, "I brought the dog specially for you."

"Why?"

"Because I know you like animals."

I couldn't figure out how he would know that about me if I didn't even know it myself. I didn't answer because I didn't know what to say. But I think he could see by my face that I was confused.

He said, "You think I don't notice what you draw in my class when it's your own choice? Eighty percent horses. Twenty percent other animals."

Oh. Horses. Right. I thought about Trudy, but I wasn't going to tell him about that. I still didn't say anything. I had one arm in front of my drawing, because I was hoping I didn't have to show it to him. Maybe he wouldn't think it was good. Maybe he would decide he was wrong. That I didn't have talent after all.

"Do you have a dog?" he asked.

I laughed that sarcastic laugh again. "My mother, take care of a dog? I can't even get her to take care of me."

"She wouldn't even let you keep a dog if you took care of it yourself?"

"She wouldn't even let me keep my little brother if I took care of him myself."

Then I realized I'd said too much and everybody was a little embarrassed, so I got up to go. I saw him reach out for my picture, so I just ditched it on the table and got out of there before he could tell me if he thought it was good or not.

Rachel followed me out. I walked fast to try to lose her, but she just walked faster and kept up.

"You like horses?" she asked. "Do you ride?"

"Uh, no. I mean, not lately. When I was little, my uncle had a farm, and I used to ride a horse out there. Trudy. But then he died. I was little."

"I ride," she said. She didn't seem to get it, that I mostly just wanted to go home. "I ride at that place out on the dunes. The Animal Ranch. You know it?"

"No," I said, and walked even faster.

By now we were walking down the front steps of the school.

"It's that place where disabled people can go to ride."

I slowed down a little. "Disabled how?"

"Physically disabled. Mostly. But they also use their horses for the Special Olympics."

When she said that, I started walking at a normal speed, and I actually looked at her face. I said, "My brother Bill has Down's Syndrome."

"Maybe he could ride," she said.

I was thinking that, too, but I didn't even want to go into

176

the whole thing about how it wouldn't be till summer at least. "I bet he'd like that."

"You could ride," she said. "I go out every Saturday and groom the horses and then we get to ride because it helps keep them trained. They have about ten volunteers our age. Because the owner's in a wheelchair. Come tomorrow. At noon. She'll let you ride."

"Oh. Tomorrow. Um. I don't think I could get my mother to drive me out there."

"My mom will drive us. We'll pick you up."

"Oh. Well, first let me ask my mom if she will."

It seemed all of a sudden like there was no getting out of this. But I didn't really want to go with Rachel and her mother. I wanted to go on my own. In case I hated every part of it and wanted to go home.

She gave me her phone number and told me to call her if I needed a lift.

Then she walked the other way, toward the bus stop.

I watched her back and thought, Is that how you make a friend? They just sort of come up and attach themselves to you, and then there you are?

It had been so long since I'd made a new friend, I really didn't remember.

I didn't ask my mom if she would drive me out to the Animal Ranch. I asked Pat.

"Okay," she said.

"That was easy."

"How hard is it supposed to be?"

"I don't know. Everything feels hard to me right now."

"I know. That's why I think this is a good idea. I like seeing you get out of the house a little more."

And that was all there was to that. I didn't exactly want to do it, but then there I was doing it. Like art club, only faster.

CHAPTER 12

Spooky

The day I showed up at the Animal Ranch was the worst possible day for a new person to be there. One of the volunteers was having a birthday, and the owner made the day a big party for her. They rode, but instead of the usual system, which is more like a big riding lesson, they were having these games on horseback. Relays and barrel races and stuff like that. And I wasn't nearly a good enough rider to do any of that. I hadn't ridden since I was, like, three.

I stood by the barn and watched them riding down this long slope to the arena, and I felt like they were all on one planet and I was on another one entirely.

Rachel hadn't even showed up yet.

"Let's just go," I said to Pat.

"I think you should at least get to know the owner first. Tell her you want to be a volunteer."

I sighed. I'd really been hoping we could just go.

I found the owner in a little office in the barn. Sitting in her wheelchair at the desk. She was about Pat's age, but with really long gray hair. It looked long enough to get caught in the wheels of the chair if she wasn't careful. Her face was friendly and soft and it was hard to be scared of her. She looked up at me. Really deep into my face, like she was memorizing me. "I'm Meg. You're the new girl? Rachel's friend?"

I think I just nodded. I guess Rachel or her mom must've called and told her I was coming.

"Here's what you can do. If you want to help. You can take Feather. She's just a yearling. Too young to be ridden. But she needs to be socialized. She's spooky. So if you'd just halter her and take her down to the arena. Just walk her around down there. That'd be a big help for your first day. You can ride next time."

"Oh. Okay."

She wheeled out into the barn aisle with me and down a few stalls and then there was Feather, leaning over the half-door of her stall. She was huge. Like the size of a draft horse. You could tell she was young but she was still just huge. Black, with a white blaze down her face and the most amazing long, thick black mane. She tossed her head when she saw us coming.

I picked up her halter and slid the stall door open just

enough so I could squeeze through. I was getting nervous, and I think the horse knew it. I wasn't afraid of Feather. I was nervous because this was that moment, that alphabet moment, when I was supposed to already know what I was doing.

"Stay on her left side," the woman said, and then I felt a little better, knowing there would be instructions. "Run one hand down her neck so she knows where you are. That's right. Now just slip the halter onto her face. Ask her to bring her head down a little. Just put one hand on top of her head . . . yeah, there, between her ears, and just gently ask her to lower her head. . . ."

Fortunately, as I followed the directions, I could tell the horse knew what she was doing. Even if I didn't.

Meg showed me how to buckle the halter under the horse's jaw, and then I opened the stall door all the way and Feather danced her way out into the barn aisle.

"Keep her attention," the woman said. "Make her pay attention to you the whole time you're out there. And don't panic if she spooks and breaks away from you. She'll only run back to the barn. But then you have to walk back and get her and try again. So try not to lose her if you can help it."

"Thanks," I said. Because I suddenly appreciated getting to stay and having something real to do.

I walked the horse out of the barn, squinting into the bright sunshine. I saw Rachel and her mother pull up. Feather reacted to the sound of the car coming close, so I gently shook the lead rope and then turned her head back to me and made her pay attention. Rachel waved at me, but I just sort of nodded my head so I wouldn't spook the horse.

I looked over to see Pat watching me. A little surprised.

"I guess I'm staying," I said.

"I guess you are."

As I walked Feather down to the arena, I looked back over my shoulder and saw the owner out in front of the barn talking to Pat.

It's actually a lot of work getting a horse to pay attention to you every second. Not physical work, but it's tiring. It reminded me in a weird way of drawing a dog. You have to be right there the whole time. You can't just go somewhere else in your head.

I learned pretty fast what made Feather feel spooky. Sudden movement, especially other horses in the arena coming up from behind her. I learned the moment when she'd see them and start to dance. And I'd have to get her attention back. Sudden loud noises, like a girl shrieking with laughter, and Feather would go straight up and come down dancing.

I had to keep my feet out from under her hooves. I learned to put one hand on her neck. That seemed to calm her.

After a while I left one hand on her most of the time. Her neck felt hot and a little damp, like she was sweating. Even though she wasn't really getting any exercise. And I could feel her heart pound—or at least I thought I could. Then I realized I probably couldn't feel her heart by touching her neck. I was probably feeling a pulse of blood going through her veins. But that's kind of like her heartbeat, too. Just a little less direct.

That's when it hit me that she was scared all the time. Even when I knew there was nothing to be scared about. She was just in this constant state of scared, and any little thing would set it off. And the fact that she was so sure something was about to set it off would set it off. Even if nothing much happened.

That's when Feather and I started to really understand each other. And that's when I started talking to her.

"See, this is just about you being scared," I said. "It isn't even about anything scary. You're totally fine, but you're so scared that you're not fine. But the only thing about you that's not fine is that you're scared. And there isn't even really anything to be scared of. But you want to run home to the barn, because you feel safe there. But there's nothing out here to hurt you, and if you just stay out here, you'll find that out. But your head's still telling you to run away. If you could just calm down and know you were okay, you'd be okay."

She was looking into my face while I talked to her. Not paying so much attention to the arena. Her face got so close to mine that I could feel the air from her nostrils puffing onto my face. She even touched my face with her fuzzy lip.

"Believe me," I said. "I'm talking from firsthand experience. You're hearing this from someone who really gets how you feel. Take it from me. If you just don't run back to the barn, everything will be fine."

I looked up to see the owner sitting in her chair by the

183

arena railing, watching us. I'd been so wrapped up in taking care of Feather, I hadn't even seen her come down. So I kept the horse's attention, all right. And I guess she kept mine.

When I was putting Feather back in the stall at the end of the day, I heard the sound of the owner's wheels in the barn aisle right outside.

"You're good with her," she said. "She responds to you."

"Thanks," I said, because I didn't know what else to say.

"Maybe when it comes time to break her, you'll consider being the first one on her back."

"I guess. If you think I'll know what to do."

"That's more than a year from now. You will if you keep coming back."

I smiled to myself because that's what they always say at the meetings. Keep coming back. I reached out to touch Feather's neck one more time. I felt bad leaving her. Even until next Saturday. Her pulse had calmed down a lot. She reached her nose out and bumped my face again, and I blew a little breath into her face, the way she blew breath into mine.

Then she started nosing around the pockets of my jeans, like I might have something for her, and when she didn't find anything, she bit at my jeans with her teeth.

"Don't let her do that," the woman said. "Pop her."

"Pop her?"

"Like this." Meg demonstrated how she wanted me to bring my open hand up under her muzzle and pop her on the nose.

But I didn't. I couldn't hit her. She was my friend.

184

Feather bit me again. This time I felt her teeth pinch a little of me right through my jeans. "Ow."

"Pop her," Meg said again. "Doesn't have to be hard. It's what her mother would do. Or any other horse. You have to teach her how you want to be treated."

I popped her gently on the nose and she threw her head back like I'd set off a bomb in her face. But then she came right back and nosed around my pockets again.

"See? She didn't hold it against you."

I saw Feather's lips pull back to bite, so I did it again. This time I barely had to touch her. She just backed off.

"You're setting boundaries with her," the woman said. "It's not enough that she likes you. She has to respect you, too. If you're going to have a good relationship."

I kissed Feather on the forehead and slipped out of her stall.

I looked at the owner and didn't know what to say. I wanted to say thank you for the day, but I couldn't quite figure out how to get started.

She said, "Your mother is great. You're lucky to have her."

That really threw me. First I thought, You know my mother? Then I thought, She couldn't. Nobody who knew my mother would say I was lucky to have her. Then it hit me. She meant Pat. She thought Pat was my mother. And why wouldn't she? How could anybody guess that my mother was sitting at home trying to stay sober while my AA sponsor drove me to the Animal Ranch?

I didn't bother to correct her. I just said, "Yeah. You're right. I'm pretty lucky."

⋰ ⋰ ⋰

On the drive home I was quiet a lot of the way. I guess I was thinking about everything that happened.

After a while I said, "I know this sounds weird. But I feel like I gave that horse a lot of good advice. Like . . . I'm not sure what I'm trying to say. Like, if only I could say stuff that smart to myself."

"What was the subject?" Pat asked.

"Fear."

"Ah. Yeah. That's a big one."

Nobody said anything for a long time. Then Pat said, "Maybe next time you get scared you can talk to yourself the same way you would talk to a spooky horse."

"That's kind of a weird idea," I said.

"Doesn't mean it wouldn't work."

"True," I said.

Sometime in the late morning on Monday, I passed my history teacher standing out in the hall. She smiled at me, and I smiled back. And then she said it.

"I hear you're quite the artist."

I just stopped in my tracks. My throat felt dry, and the first time I opened my mouth, nothing happened, so I tried again. "Who told you that?"

"Joe Werther was talking about you in the teachers' lounge. Showing around the picture you drew of his Irish setter. He just couldn't say enough about it. I thought it was a wonderful picture, but he said you couldn't really appreciate it unless you knew his dog. He said you really captured her, right down to the expression on her face. He thinks you're quite talented."

I'm not sure what I said. Probably nothing at all. I was just too stunned to say anything, I think. If I did say anything, I was probably mumbling, and I bet it sounded stupid.

The bell rang, which meant I was late to math, but I didn't go straight to math. I went to Mr. Werther's room. The door was closed, because class had started, but I opened it and peeked in. He saw me and looked up and stopped talking. Got up and came to the door to see what I wanted. I almost ran away. But I thought about Feather, and I stayed.

Mr. Werther smiled at me. "I wish you hadn't run out so fast on Friday."

"You told all my other teachers I was a good artist?"

"I'm sorry. Was it a secret?"

Then I laughed. I couldn't help it. "Yeah—I mean, no. Of course not. Thanks."

We both just stood there a second, and then he said, "Where are you supposed to be this period?"

"Oh crap. Math. I knew there was something I was forgetting."

I ran there as fast as I could. The whole way, I could feel I still had this weird little smile going on. I couldn't make it go away. Maybe I didn't really try.

I walked home with Rachel at the end of the day. She wanted to know when I rode before, so I told her about Trudy.

I said, "Back when my uncle Jim was alive, he had this farm. It was about three hours from here. In the valley. I remember it was really hot there, but I used to love to go. And he had this horse named Trudy. This big old palomino. I was only about three or four, but she was so gentle they could just put me up on there bareback. She didn't even need a bridle. I just held on to her halter rope. I loved her so much, I never went in the house. I mean not if I could help it. When I wasn't riding her I used to pick apples and pears from the trees— Uncle Jim had fruit trees—and feed them to her over the fence. But then Uncle Jim died. He had to go in for this surgery that was supposed to be no big deal. Or maybe they just told me that so I wouldn't worry. Anyway, he died."

"That's sad," she said.

It wasn't that sad, really, because I was so little and I really didn't know my uncle Jim very well. He always looked like a stranger to me and I think I was a little bit afraid of him. But I didn't say that, because I didn't know her that well yet, and I didn't want her to think I was weird.

"What's really sad," I said, "is that when I got old enough, I asked my aunt if I could go out to the farm and see Trudy. She said Trudy died. Some idiot neighbors were out hunting drunk and they shot her and she died."

"On purpose? Or did they think she was a deer or something?"

"I don't know. I didn't ask. I was so busy thinking how

nobody told me. Like, how could they not get that I would want to know? After that I didn't want anything to do with horses. You know how some people are." I was hoping she would know, so I wouldn't have to explain it.

"No, how?"

"You know. Some people just don't want to get near anything that could hurt."

"That's everybody. Isn't it?"

"Not really. Some people can have a dog, and then if the dog dies, they get another one. Other people, they say, No, that's it. Too painful. Not going through that again."

"I would get another dog," she said.

"I think I would, too," I said. "Now."

"What changed?"

"Pretty much everything."

My mom was driving me crazy.

I felt so bad saying that, but I had to say it, or I'd have been even crazier.

It hit a kind of all-time low that Friday night.

I got home from school, and there she was, meeting me at the door, all sort of . . . eager. Perky. Or something.

It sounds like a good thing, I know. But when she did it, somehow it felt really wrong. Really forced, like it made her nervous to do it, so it made me nervous to have to be there and watch.

She'd had her hair straightened and dyed it blond. Or bleached it, or whatever. It sounds trashy, but it was just the opposite. She was trying for a more sophisticated look. She never wore her robe around the house anymore. She got dressed. And did her nails and put on makeup and everything, which I think comes off as sort of weird if you go to all that trouble and then just . . . you know . . . stay home.

I think it's because she was trying to throw off the whole trailer-trash image. I really hate to use words like that about my own mother, but sometimes you just have to say what you mean. I also think it was because she was always scratching around for something—anything—to do.

She said, "It's Friday. T.G.I.F., huh?"

"Right," I said. "Whatever." I just couldn't do perky with her. Not even when I tried.

"I thought we could order a pizza. Wouldn't that be fun?"

"Uh. Yeah. Pizza would be good."

"And maybe a game of Monopoly and then we can stay up and watch Letterman."

I swear it was all I could do not to roll my eyes. I was thinking, I'm not your gal pal. Can't you have fun on your own? I was thinking, I don't like Letterman, I like Leno. But of course I kept my mouth shut.

I feel bad saying all this, because before I was bitching about how she was never a real mother. So it sounds like I'm just miserable and complaining either way. But there was something more to it. I just couldn't put my finger on it. It's like, when she's acting like a real mother, it isn't exactly real.

But I was trying hard to be supportive. Every time I started to lose it with her, I just thought, She's trying, so you try, too. She's reaching out, so the least you can do is meet her partway.

All I said was, "Double cheese and pepperoni?"

"Perfect!"

I took the phone in my room and locked the door and ordered the damn pizza. Then I called Pat.

"Pat," I said, "she's driving me batty. She wants to have a freaking slumber party. I don't want to do this, Pat."

She said, "Don't take this wrong, okay? Hear this the way it's intended. What are you afraid of?"

"Nothing."

"Sounds to me like you're scared to death of something."

"Really? I don't know. I mean, I don't think so."

"Think it over before you answer," she said. "You know how that fear thing can be."

I breathed in and out real deeply for a minute, and some of the crazy feeling started to clear away. Next thing you know, I was answering her question.

"I'm afraid if I let her get close to me and really talk to me, she's going to tell me how sorry she is and ask me to forgive her."

"And you're not ready to forgive her."

"I guess I should be, huh?"

"Honey, if you told me everything between you and your mom was water under the bridge, I'd know you'd gone back to lying to me. It takes years to look at all that stuff from a different perspective. It's a whole long process. It's not just something you up and do because you figure you're supposed

191

to. Oh, you can say 'I forgive you' to someone. But real forgiveness—that's a life's work for most people."

"So what do I do?"

She thought about it a minute. "Try cutting her a little slack on one tiny thing. One thing that's small enough you really can let it go. Volunteer something. Maybe she'll take that as a down payment."

"Okay," I said. "I'm going in. Wish me luck."

I was sitting across the Monopoly board from her, and every now and then she would belch, and I was trying not to pass judgment. I'd had two and a half slices of pizza and she'd killed the whole rest of the damn thing. She even finished my crusts. I never saw anybody eat like that in my whole life. So much for my midnight snack. But I said nothing.

She was rolling the dice in her hand, not quite managing to throw them, and she looked up from the game, right into my eyes. Like a frog she was about to dissect. "How was school?"

I refused to lie. "I hate school."

She looked disappointed. "Why?"

"Did you used to like school?"

"No. I hated it."

"Well?"

That's when it hit me. Something else that scared me. Every time she tried to get to know me, I kept seeing this person who was, like, a total stranger. Even scarier, it seemed almost like this someone was even a stranger to her. It's like she was trying to get to know me and herself at the same time. And it was weird, and upsetting, because she was my mother. I recognized her voice, and I was used to the shape of her sitting around the house. But this was like a conversation with an adult stranger.

And then, underneath that, was something even weirder and scarier. This wasn't a stranger at all, and I knew it. This was my real mom, and part of me almost remembered her. We just hadn't seen each other for such an incredibly long time.

I tried to shake it off.

I said, "I'm sorry I was so hard on you about the job thing."

She just froze, her hand holding the dice. Yes, amazingly, she still had not thrown the damn dice. See how unnatural this whole thing was? She just kept looking at me.

I said, "I know it's weird and scary to have to think about going out and getting a job. So . . . I'm sorry I came down on you so hard about it."

On the one hand, I'm not sure I would have thought to say that if Pat hadn't suggested it. But at the same time it felt like something that just bubbled up all on its own.

"Thank you, Cynthia."

I closed my eyes and prayed Pat was right. That this would hold her for a while. I said, "Mom, throw the dice, okay?"

After Letterman, she wanted me to stay up and talk to her. And, I mean, there has to be a limit. I can try my best, I can really bend over backwards for her, but after a while it gets to be like abuse.

"Mom. It's late. I'm tired."

"Oh, come on. It'll be fun."

Yeah. Right. More fun than a barrel of scorpions. I said, "Why don't you just go to sleep?"

All of a sudden she looked at me like she was about to cry. "I haven't been able to sleep much. It's really hard. I just really wanted the company."

"Oh." Thank you so much. For making me feel like crap about it. "Want me to make you a glass of warm milk before I go to bed?"

"That would be lovely, Cynthia. Thank you."

I got the feeling that she didn't care so much about the milk as getting me to stay up a little bit longer.

I said a little prayer that she'd stay in the living room and leave me alone while I heated it up. She followed me into the kitchen like an old dog. Sat at the table and stared at me. I was really at the end of my rope with the staring thing.

I stood at the stove and kept my back to her.

She said, "I know it broke your heart when I sent Bill away."

It hit my back and just sort of bounced off me. I wouldn't turn around. I wouldn't answer. I would not forgive her for that. Not that. It was wrong of her to ask me to forgive her for that. It was asking too much.

I just kept stirring the damn milk. I didn't know what else I was supposed to do.

"I'm sorry," she said.

I took down a glass and poured the milk into it. Set it on the table for her. Made sure not to look her in the eye.

"Let's just work on getting him back here," I said. "That would be a good next step. You just stay sober and bring him back here for the summer and that'll go a long way."

"I won't let you down," she said.

She had to say it to my back. She had to call it after me fast as I was going off to bed and glorious privacy at last.

Next time I went to art club, Rachel was out sick, and that guy, the only guy in art club, tried to follow me home. Well, walk me home. I guess I shouldn't make it sound like he was stalking me. He just started talking to me on the way out. Then next thing I knew I was, like, halfway home and he was still there.

He was one of those guys whose face looked good enough, but since he carried himself like a nerd, you couldn't really say he was handsome. But he was okay, except his ears were a little too big.

I still didn't know his name. And he didn't tell me, because I guess he thought I knew. So it seemed way too late to tell him I didn't.

He talked about art, and I could hardly get a word in edgewise. I just kept looking at the sidewalk and nodding. Then he was quiet for a minute, but I still didn't get any words in because I had no idea what to say. Before I could think of anything, he asked me if I had a boyfriend. I stopped walking and so did he.

I looked up at him, but by then he was looking down at the sidewalk. It seemed like we were taking turns with that.

"I'm not sure," I said.

"How can you not be sure?"

"Well. There's this guy. But I'm not really sure if he's my boyfriend. But if I had a boyfriend, it would definitely be him. Because we've been through a lot together. Know what I mean?"

He was still looking at the sidewalk. I looked past him and saw Snake walking down the street behind us. I felt really glad to see him. Like he was rescuing me. I waved really big and motioned for him to catch up.

The kid whose name I didn't know said, "Okay, then, thanks anyway." And he walked off before Snake could catch up to us.

I looked at Snake, and I think he could see by the look on my face that I was glad to see him.

"I wasn't spying on you," he said. "I just wanted to see if I could catch you on your way home from school."

"I didn't think you were spying. I was happy to see you. I think that guy was trying to ask me out. But I told him if I had a boyfriend it would be you. And then when you were there, it was perfect timing."

He smiled and looked kind of shy, and I could see that he had been worried. I could tell by the relief on his face when he got to stop.

He said, "Want to go for an ice cream?"

Not going home sounded like the most wonderful plan ever. I couldn't believe I hadn't thought of it myself.

On the way down to the ice cream place he said, "You never really told me much about what happened to you. You know. After I took off."

"Oh. Probably because it was all bad."

"You don't have to if you don't want."

"No, it's okay. Nanny and Grampop came and got Bill from the hospital. I never even got to see him. Or them. They didn't even poke their heads in my room and say 'hi.' I had to go to court. Got probation, thank God. Because I'd never been in trouble before. I think they thought it was all your fault. Even though I kept trying to tell them I was the brains behind the outfit. No offense."

"I knew what you meant."

"Anyway, you know, older boy and all. I guess they figured you had me doing stuff that was unlike me. Little did they know."

"So you just have to see a probation officer?"

"No, they also make me go to AA meetings. And they make me take pee tests, so they know what I've been doing."

"So, are you, like, just dying to get that over with so you can go back to being yourself?"

"Yes and no," I said. "I'll be happy to be done with probation, all right."

And then we were at the ice cream place, and there was no line. I got one of those chocolate cones where they fill it up with a giant spiral of soft-serve chocolate and then dip it in a chocolate coating that freezes on. Snake got vanilla, which seemed weird. Why would anyone like vanilla? And why didn't I know he did?

We sat outside.

I said, "I'm trying not to go back to that. At all. I figure I'll keep going to the meetings and try to stick with it. Even after I don't really have to."

I was all ready to hear him say something like, What the hell is that all about? Or, Wow, they really brainwash you, huh? That's the way I thought someone from the outside would see it.

"Good for you," he said.

"You really mean that?"

"Absolutely. I was kind of worried about it. You know. That you'd turn out . . ."

"Like my mom?"

He put his hands—ice cream cone and all—in front of his face. Like pretend defense. "I'm not running down your mom. Not after what happened to Richie." We both laughed a little. It was funny but kind of uncomfortable, too. Then he said, "But seriously, I was worried."

"Did it seem like I was that bad?"

I could tell I was putting him on the spot. He didn't want to answer that. He stumbled around a little. "I don't know. Maybe. I mean, I don't know how bad it has to be. You know. To be bad. It just seemed . . . But I don't know, I could be wrong, too. I'm not trying to judge you."

"No, it's okay. I want you to. I mean, I want to hear this.

198

Because I was so sure it wasn't that bad. But now I'm thinking maybe I was looking at it wrong."

"Those bad habits have a funny way of making you look at them wrong."

I wondered how he knew. Snake didn't drink, so far as I knew. I'd never seen him drink.

I said, "Here's the really weird part. This will blow you away. Now my mom is going to the meetings and not drinking."

"You're shittin' me."

I held up one hand like I was in court. God forbid. "May God strike me dead if I'm lying."

"That sounds weird. I mean . . . is it weird? Or is it okay?"

"Well. There are okay parts. Like, if she stays sober, we're going to get Bill back for the whole summer. I'm looking forward to that so much I can hardly stand it. I was scared he was going to forget me." I was surprised I said that. I didn't know I was about to say something so honest. "But mostly it's weird."

"No way. That kid would never forget you. You're his whole world." I thought that was a nice thing to say. "I know you really love that kid. I think it's nice, too. I know I was kind of nasty about it. But I was just being selfish. It was nice. It's like I knew you didn't care about school, or your mom, or me, but it was nice to see that you cared about something." He licked some melted ice cream off the cone and the side of his hand. We were both quiet a minute. Probably a little embarrassed. Then he said, "What's the downside?"

"Of what?"

"You said there were bad parts to your mom not drinking."

"Oh. That. Yeah, lots of them. She comes to my meetings, which makes it really hard to be myself. And she notices me now, and everything that happens in the house, and I feel like I'm being watched all the time. And she wants to be taken care of. She's feeling all . . . you know . . . like . . . *fragile* or something. And she wants me around all the time and she wants me to cook for her and bring her things and watch TV with her. It's exhausting. It's like having a kid. I swear, now I know what it feels like to be a mother. Well, I already did, because of Bill. But he was easy, compared to my mom. She's really tough to raise. Boy, I swear I could use a vacation."

"How about just a little vacation? How about if Friday I pick you up and we'll go see a movie? There're about three good things playing downtown. I'll even let you pick the movie. Think she'd let you go?"

"It's not up to her. I'm the mother, remember?"

"Does that mean yes?"

"Yes."

"Cool."

We were pretty much done with our ice cream by then, so he walked me home. We didn't really talk much on the way. But it wasn't weird or anything. We just walked along and didn't need to keep filling up the air with chatter.

When we got to the end of my driveway he said, "I keep meaning to say something about that letter you gave me."

"Yeah, I wondered." My stomach felt a little scared.

"I've been meaning to say don't feel so bad. We both pretty

much screwed up big-time. I mean, I don't think even *you* could make that big a mess all by yourself. But anyway, thanks for what you said."

Then he walked away. Didn't try to kiss me or hug me goodbye or anything. Just turned around and walked home. Wherever that was.

CHAPTER 13

The Kind You Get
to Pick Out Yourself

Nanny and Grampop still hadn't written me back.

I called Pat to talk about it.

She said trust was hard. We break somebody's trust a few times and we can't get it back just like that. It takes time and effort. We have to give them time to see that we really are serious about changing.

She said if I wanted, she'd talk to them for me. Put in a good word.

"Thanks," I said. "But I'd like to try one more time on my own."

Then I got off the phone and sat there wondering what I could say to them that I hadn't already said last time. That's when it hit me, and I felt really stupid that it had never hit me before.

I called Pat back. I said, "I never made amends to Nanny and Grampop."

She said, "Bingo."

"You thought of that already? Why didn't you tell me?"

"I was hoping you would think of it on your own."

"If I sit down and write them a letter for my amends, can I read it to you first?"

"Sure," she said.

And then I got off the phone because I had a lot of work to do.

I spent the whole evening working on it and took it over to Pat's the next day.

She just sat quietly and listened while I read it to her. Which was really embarrassing. But I did it anyway.

"Dear Nanny and Grampop,

"I think I should have written this letter to you a long time ago. It's funny how the more I go along, the more I look back on what came before, like things I did in the past, and see them in a different way. So when it hits me that I owe amends to someone, I think it's because I'm finally able to see what really happened.

"I think when I took Bill I felt almost like he

belonged to me. Because I felt like I was the only one who really cared about him. But now I know it isn't enough to care about him. You have to be able to *take* care of him. I don't know how I thought I was going to do that.

"I guess there were a lot of things I didn't think through.

"I just know that I shouldn't have stolen him in the middle of the night, no matter how much I love him and how much I wanted him back. I also know I took a big risk driving with him. So I can look back at the way I loved him then and see that it wasn't a very good kind of love if I was willing to take that much of a chance with his safety. I'm sorry I couldn't see that at the time.

"I'm not trying to steal him now. I'm trying to earn him.

"Whether you believe me or not, I'm trying to learn to be the kind of person who can take care of him. Just for the summer at first. Mom is trying, too.

"I know I've let you down before, and there's nothing I can say now that will magically make you trust me. I know that, and I really understand. Maybe if I were you, I wouldn't trust me, either. So if you want to watch me for a while to see if I really mean it, that's okay.

"I just need to ask again if you'll read letters to Bill for me if I write them. Because I'm just really scared that he'll forget all about me. Here I am working so hard to be able to get him back and I worry that he won't even remember me when the time comes. I don't know if you're not answering me because it would take time to read to him, or because you think I don't deserve it. Maybe I don't. But Bill does. He deserves to still have a sister.

"When you came to Arizona and picked Bill up at the hospital, I was really hurt because you didn't even come in and see me. I think I was mad about that for a long time. But now when I look back I'm mad at myself, not you. Now it's hard to blame you for being too upset to talk to me right then.

"So no matter what you decide about the letters, I just want to say I'm sorry for what I did. And I'm not just saying it to try to get something from you. I really mean it.

Love, Cynthia"

When I was done reading, I looked at Pat and she just nodded. So I walked it down to the mailbox, dropped it in, and hoped for the best.

The next day—the day I was supposed to go to the movies with Snake—my mom and I had another fight. I don't know how I could be so stupid, to start thinking we never would.

It was when I told her I was going to be gone all evening. I mean, it's not like she needed a babysitter or anything. I didn't think we'd get into a big fight about it.

"Who's the boy?" she wanted to know.

I wasn't expecting that. Where did she get off all of a sudden? Acting like she could tell me what to do when I'd been running the show all this time. "Why? What does it matter?"

She said, "If you have a boyfriend, I ought to know about him."

I said, "I'm not even sure he *is* my boyfriend. We're just going to a movie."

"What's his name?"

I didn't want to lie, because of the honesty thing in the program. If I told a lie, I'd just have to make up for it later. So I said, "His name is Morris." That was true.

"Morris Rooney? That 'Snake' kid?"

"Yeah, what about it?"

"I don't want you seeing that boy, Cynnie." It made me mad that she called me Cynnie, like I'd just gotten younger all of a sudden.

"Why not? What's wrong with Snake?"

"I am not letting you go out with that boy you ran off with."

"Nothing happened with us, anyway. I'm not sleeping with him." I could see she didn't believe me. I was starting to get really mad. It just came on me. Right there, right while it was happening, I could tell how I felt about something. It felt like this big thing, this force, something I couldn't control. It reminded me of Snake's car, going into that last spin. I didn't know how to stop it.

I said, "Look, you can't have it both ways. First you want me to stay home and take care of you and do all this stuff you just don't feel ready to do. Now you want to tell me who I can see. Make up your mind. You're either the mother or you're not."

The room got real quiet. After a while she said, "Fine. Do what you want. You're a big girl."

I went off into my room to get ready for my date. Thinking I would've liked it better the other way around. If she'd decided to be the mother.

When we got home the house was all dark. I figured she'd turned in early. Ever since she'd gotten sober she had this habit of going to bed when all else failed. Sleep or no sleep. But some other little part of me was still expecting something bad.

I think Snake caught on to that, because he said, "Want me to come in with you?"

"Yeah, maybe for just a minute."

He waited in the dark living room while I looked into her bedroom. But there was nobody home in there. The bed was made—by me, of course—and there was no one in it. That little thing in my stomach got bigger.

I heard Snake's voice saying, "Hey. Cynnie."

I knew exactly what to expect.

I found him in the dining room and turned on a light, and

there it was. The whole ugly scene. My mom was lying face-down on the carpet. Passed out. I hoped just passed out. I leaned over her and put a hand on her back until I could feel she was breathing. Then I breathed, too. She was drooling out of one side of her mouth onto the carpet. It was completely disgusting. The bottle she'd been carrying across the room when she fell was lying beside her hand, and it had been open and spilled whatever was left. I could see the dark wet place on the carpet. Worse yet, I could smell it.

You could tell she really fell hard, not just crumpled up, because the gin was thrown in a long line, about a foot forward from where she landed. Part of me hoped she hadn't hurt herself, but only part of me. I know that's a terrible thing to say.

I stood over her and watched my dream of our summer with Bill flying away. I was so furious, I swear I almost kicked her. That was my first thought. To haul off and kick her as hard as I could. Then I thought about throwing ice water on her. I hated her more at that moment than I think I ever had before. I just couldn't think of anything bad enough to punish her for doing this to me.

But I didn't do anything to her. I just felt really tired.

Snake said, "Got any carpet cleaner?"

"There should be some under the sink."

I sat down on a dining room chair. Hardly even feeling I was doing it. I felt like an inner tube after somebody stuck a knife in the side of it. I was going down fast.

Snake came back in with a roll of paper towels and a can

of the carpet stuff. He started blotting up as much of the gin as he could.

"I should probably do that," I said. "My mom, my mess." But I didn't put much behind it.

"I just thought it would be better if I did, because . . . you know." I didn't, actually. "Because it smells, and you're trying to stay away from that and all."

"Oh. Thanks."

"Besides, I'm good at this. I got a lot of practice, cleaning up after my dad."

"Your dad drinks?"

He made a big noise of air rushing out of him. "Hoo. You have no idea. He makes your mom look like a social drinker. And he's mean when he drinks, too. You just look at him wrong and he'll beat the crap out of you. This is nothing. A little spilled booze. He used to puke on the carpet. Or he'd wake up in his own piss. And then just get up and go on with his day like it never happened. So I did a lot of carpet cleaning. Not because I owed him anything. I just didn't want to smell it. I didn't want to live like that, you know?"

I sat there with my head in my hands. I was listening, though. And taking in how strange it was to find this out now. But if people don't want to tell you something, then you won't know.

I said, "Is that why you don't drink?"

"Yeah."

I still had my head in my hands but I could hear the aerosol sound of the carpet cleaner being sprayed. I was thinking how strange it was, that Snake reacted to his dad by never drinking, and I reacted to my mom by following in her footsteps. Sometimes life is too complicated and backwards, and it's so hard to make sense of things. I tried to think what Pat would say about that. She'd probably say, It doesn't matter why. It matters what you're going to do about it.

Snake said, "I'd leave this on till morning. If you vacuum it up in the morning, it should be fine."

I took my head out of my hands and looked at him. Really looked at him. "Thank you," I said. Like I meant it. Because I did.

"Want me to help you get her in bed?"

"No. Thanks. I think she should spend the night right here."

"Need company?"

"No. I really appreciate what you did. Seriously. This would've been so much harder if you hadn't been here. But I just need to go to bed. You understand, right?" I knew he would. Because of that night we ran away. He was upset, and he didn't want to talk.

"Yeah. It's okay."

But then, just as he was walking to the door, I started wondering why I was chasing him away. It's like as soon as I knew he would understand my wanting to be alone—just like that, no questions—I didn't really need him to go.

"You know what?" I said. "Maybe you could just stay a few minutes. Go sit in the kitchen for a minute, okay? I'll be right in."

I ran into my room and got my drawing pad and a pencil. When I got back to the kitchen he was sitting there waiting. I sat across from him. Past him and through the kitchen door I could see my mom's feet sprawled out on the carpet. So I just looked at Snake instead.

"You don't mind, do you?" He was looking like a hero to me. Not that I would have said that. It would have sounded wrong. I just mean, a hero, like . . . strong. Like someone who can be strong when you need him to be. And I wanted to get that down in a drawing.

"No, I don't mind."

At first we tried talking a little, but I was concentrating too hard to really keep up my end of the conversation. So then we just sat there and I drew his face and we didn't talk. That was sort of what I liked about Snake, anyway. We didn't always have to talk.

After a while I looked at the clock and saw I'd been drawing for almost forty-five minutes.

"Are you getting tired of posing?" I asked him.

"I'm okay," he said.

But I looked at the drawing and decided I could go on for hours or just stop now. It didn't really matter. The important part—the hero part—was already down on paper.

I turned it around and showed it to him.

He reached out and took it in his hands and looked at it for a long time. Neither one of us said anything. After a while, though, I really wanted to know if he liked it.

"Do you think it looks like you?"

"Yes and no," he said, and at first I was disappointed. "It's not what I see when I look in the mirror. It's like when I close my eyes, I want to think I look like this. But then when I look in the mirror I see something that isn't this good. It's almost like you drew what I'm *trying* to be. Do you have any idea what I'm talking about?"

"Yeah. I think so." And I wasn't disappointed anymore.

"Is this really how you see me?"

"I guess it must be."

"Can I keep this?"

"Sure. Of course you can."

I walked him to the door and gave him a little kiss and thanked him again and said good night. Feeling grateful because I had at least one friend back.

When I closed the door and turned around there was my mom, passed out on the carpet.

I went into my room and flopped down on the bed. Then for some reason I thought about Pat, that night up in the tree house. When I was almost as drunk as my mom was right now. How she held me and rocked me and let me cry all over her shirt and covered me with her jacket.

I got the crocheted afghan off the back of the couch and went back into the dining room where my mom was and covered her up with it so she wouldn't be cold. And I sat there with her all night, just to make sure she'd be okay. Not because she deserved it, exactly. More because I hadn't deserved it, either, when Pat did it for me.

In the morning I woke up on the carpet and my mom was nowhere around. My eyes felt burny, and I was a little sick to my stomach from not sleeping much, and from being upset. I found my mom sitting at the kitchen table drinking instant coffee. She looked pretty awful.

I was thinking, We can still sober her up in time. It's not summer yet. We'll get her back on track in time for summer.

I said, "You better get ready. We're going to that Sunday morning meeting." She never looked up at me. I said, "This happens to a lot of people. It happened to me. You just have to start all over."

She lit a cigarette. She said, "I'm not as strong as you are."

I sat down next to her. I was trying to get her to look at me, but she never did. I said, "I *need* you to be. I need you to be my mother."

She started to cry.

I went to the meeting anyway. Just before I left I asked if she was sure she wasn't going. She said, "I can't, Cynnie. I'm not strong like you." She said it so quiet, I had to ask her to say it again. Then I wished I hadn't.

Pat took me to the IHOP after the meeting, and I ordered a big stack of pancakes. I thought if I ate enough I might feel numb.

I said, "It's my fault. I yelled at her. I said she couldn't tell me what to do because she was still making me be the mother. I hurt her feelings."

Pat clicked her tongue and shook her head. "Can't make

somebody else get drunk, Cynthia. They're either going to do it when something goes wrong or they're not. Now for the bad news: Can't make somebody else stay sober, either."

"She says she's not as strong as I am."

"Maybe that's true."

"I used to think I could take care of everything. I thought I was like a momma lion—I'd stand up for myself and for Bill and everything would be okay."

"Maybe it still will be. Maybe it'll just take longer than you thought." Then she used an expression I never heard before. One of those program sayings. She said, "If she'll drink over anything, she'll drink over anything." At first I didn't get it. Then I did. Mom got drunk because we had a fight. Or maybe it was because of the pressure of trying to get ready for the responsibility of having Bill around. Or because even thinking about Bill made her feel guilty. Anyway, if there's anything in the whole world that can knock you off your program, then you'll get knocked off it. Something will come along sooner or later.

I said, "Why can't she get it, Pat? I wanted her to get it." I wasn't sure if I could cry and eat pancakes at the same time. I was about to find out.

"Maybe you really are stronger."

"I wanted her to get better. She's my mom. It's not fair."

"No, I guess it's not. Some people get it. Some don't."

"We can't just give up on her," I said. "You didn't give up on me after one slip."

Pat was quiet for a minute. Too long a minute if you'd

asked me. Then she said, "But you got up the next day and went back to the meetings. You didn't just fold up and say you weren't strong enough to try again."

"There's got to be something we can do for her."

"Only if she gets back to a place where she's willing to do something for herself. If that happens, we'll be a hundred percent behind her again. But until then, you really can't help her. And if I were you, I'd accept that."

"Accept that . . . I have to wait till she's ready to try?"

"And that she might never get ready." At first I thought she was being unsympathetic, but when I looked up she looked at me like her heart was breaking on my behalf. "I'm sorry," she said. "I know it's hard to watch somebody you love fall away."

That's when I started to cry. I couldn't bring myself to say I loved her, but Pat had said it for me. "I thought we could be like a real family. I thought Bill could come home. Now how will I ever see him? I thought we'd get custody of him again."

"Here's the important question," she said. "Are you going to go back to getting drunk and acting crazy and messing up your life because she disappointed you like this?"

"No. Of course not. That wouldn't fix anything."

"Congratulations," she said. "You have officially stopped growing up to be just like your mother." Before I could even really take that in, she said, "Maybe *you* could get custody of Bill."

"Yeah? In what universe?"

"Maybe in this one, when you're eighteen."

215

"*Eighteen?*" That seemed like forever. Like my next life-time. It was more than three years away.

"If you had four years sober, and you had a job. Maybe go to college at night. I'd be willing to go to court with you. Vouch for your character. I think you'd make a great guardian. You're still the momma lion type. You protect the people you love."

"How could I work and go to school and take care of him all at the same time?"

She shook a bunch of Tabasco sauce on her eggs, like that might help her think about this hard problem. "Maybe you could rent a room in my house, get a babysitter in the deal that way."

I wanted to say thank you but I was still crying some and the words got stuck. I'd say it later, and she'd understand why I hadn't said it before. "That still sounds hard."

"It will be. But it'd be something to work for. I mean, Bill's worth it. Right?"

"Absolutely. Bill. He's worth anything." It still seemed a long way off.

"And you're worth it."

"Me?"

"Yeah, you."

"How did I get into this?"

"How can we keep you out of it? It's your program. It's your life. Maybe you'll get Bill down the road. Meantime, you're working for a better life for you. You're worth it. Right?"

I'd never really thought about that. "You think I am?"

"I know you are. I just want to know if *you* know you are."

I said, "You know, Pat, you're more like my mother than my mother is."

She said, "Well, it works like that sometimes. Blood family, that's something we get dealt. Sometimes we get a bad hand. Not much way around it. You just have to grow up and get more family. The kind you get to pick out yourself."

When I got home the phone rang. It was Nanny.

She said, "Bill wants to talk to you."

Next thing I knew, I could hear his voice on the phone.

So I talked to him. And sang with him. And asked questions to see if I could get him to say any new words. He'd been starting to say new words right around the time my phone card ran out.

After about ten minutes Nanny came back on the line. "If you want to call once a week," she said, "for about ten minutes . . . Grampop says he'll pay for it."

"You're kidding." That might have been the wrong thing to say, but I was truly amazed. "I mean . . . what I meant to say . . . can I talk to him? So I can say thank you?"

"He's taking a nap, hon."

Nanny hadn't called me "hon" in as long as I could remember.

"Well, when he wakes up, tell him I said thanks, okay?" It hit me that maybe Grampop was sitting right there. He wasn't very good at stuff like hearing thank you. But that was okay, because I still remembered how that used to feel.

Next time I went to a meeting I shared something funny. It didn't used to be funny. It used to be something that scared the crap out of me, but it got funnier after a few months went by.

I said, "When I first got here I was scared that I was going to change so fast and so much that I wouldn't even know myself. I was afraid I wouldn't be me anymore." Everybody laughed. Because they all knew. They knew what I meant, but they also knew how crazy it was. Because you always change slower than you want to, and after a while you realize that part of you doesn't change at all.

It's a hard thing to explain, but in some ways if you're broken, you're always broken. In some ways. It's like the difference between a china mug that's lying in pieces on your floor or one that's been carefully glued back together: it might not look as pretty as a brand-new one, and you might have to be a little more careful with it, but at least you can drink out of it. It works. I'm not sure I can explain it any better than that. But the really cool thing is, in that room, I didn't have to explain it. They all got it. Because they're all like me.

That's the other thing that seems funny now. How I thought maybe I was the only one.

When I was done sharing I looked around the room. I was remembering when I first got here. I couldn't stand Pat and I didn't want anyone to talk to me. Now I looked around at the people. They were mostly people I would have thought were dorky a year ago. They were all different ages. Some had been there when I showed up, like Pat and Zack and Phyllis and

Tom. Some were new people with less time than me. Some people I'd known were gone. Fallen away like my mom. Some people fall away. It's like you can save yourself, but you can't save them. But *they* can save them. But sometimes they don't, and it's hard to understand why.

I thought, This is not a bad family. Better than the blood family I got dealt.

I thought, Me and Pat and Bill. That might not be bad. I figured at least it was something worth working for. I figured maybe I was worth it.

After I got home I called Zack. I know. That's really weird. Because I'd just been at a meeting with him. But there are some things I still could never say with somebody like him staring me right in the face while I talked.

I said, "Look, do me a favor and just listen, okay? I just need you to listen to this. I've been thinking a lot lately about how you said you always liked me. And I think I knew that, even way back then. And when you're not used to people liking you, you sort of make it too big a deal, you know? Like it can't just be what it is. It has to be everything. I don't think I'm explaining it right. Anyway, I just called to tell you I love you, okay? Just love you, just like that, not like you have to do something special, I just do, okay?" I waited, but nothing happened. "Zack?"

"You told me to just listen."

"Oh. Yeah. I'm done now. Say something."

"I love you, too," he said. "You're a good kid."

"Am I really?"

"Yeah. You really are. And the more you let that tough-kid outside thing start to fall apart, the more the good-kid inside thing shows through. It's the coolest thing to watch."

I said, "I gotta go now, thanks, bye."

Then I lay there on my bed and cried for a long time. Not really in a bad way, though. If a thing like that could possibly make sense. Not like I was falling apart or like everything was awful. More like there was just a lot of stuff in there that needed to actually finally come out.

CHAPTER 14

Momma Lion

Right after I celebrated my one-year AA birthday, it was a long holiday weekend, and I got to take the bus to Redlands to see Nanny and Grampop. And, of course, Bill.

I left on Friday afternoon, and my mom was slumped over on the couch with a bottle on the coffee table in front of her and a cigarette in her hand. That worried me. She was never supposed to have a cigarette in her hand. She was supposed to put it in the ashtray in between drags. Every time. I thought I had her all trained.

"Mom," I said. She acted like she didn't even hear me. Maybe she didn't. "Mom." I took the cigarette out of her hand, and she looked up. She was really smashed.

"What?"

"Where is this supposed to go?"

"Right. I know."

"It's important. I'm going to be gone for three days. You can't forget. Remember why? Remember why it's so important not to forget?"

She thought about it a long time. Like this was a real brainteaser. "So I don't burn the house down." Her words were mushing all together.

"Right. Don't forget."

I knew Snake was waiting in the driveway to take me to the bus station, but I really wanted to call Pat. I stuck my head out the door and gave Snake a little signal, that I'd just be a minute. He caught it and nodded.

I dialed Pat's number by heart.

"Thought you'd be gone by now," she said.

"I'm just leaving. Pat, can you look in on my mom while I'm gone? I know we said to just not worry, but—"

"Sure," she said. "It's no trouble."

"Thanks, Pat. Make sure she eats something, okay? Sometimes she doesn't eat. Maybe heat her up some soup or something."

"Cynthia. We've been over this. She's home alone all the time. She'll be fine. But I'll stick my head in, just so you can stop worrying and enjoy your trip."

"Thanks, Pat."

"You gonna talk to your grandparents?"

"Yeah. I really am."

"Scared?"

"A little."

"You'll be strong. I know you will, Momma Lion. Call me collect if you need to."

"Okay. I have to go, Pat. Thanks."

I hung up the phone. I looked at my mom again. She was all fallen over sideways on the couch. But at least her cigarette was in the ashtray.

"Bye, Mom," I said. No answer. "I'll be back Monday night." Nothing. "I love you, Mom." Nothing. But at least I said it.

Snake sat in the bus station with me and held my hand while I waited.

"It's a little scary," I said.

"Think they'll fight you?"

"I don't know. I think they'll be mad. It's a little weird, telling your own family you'll be in court in a custody case in three years. I'm not sure how you say a thing like that."

"Just take a big deep breath and say it, I guess."

"I guess."

Then they announced that my bus to Redlands was boarding, so we got up and Snake carried my duffel bag all the way to the door, and then he gave me a big long hug. He was a good hugger. There was something solid about his hugs. You knew he was really in there.

"I'll miss you," he said, and gave me a little kiss.

When I looked up this older lady was smiling at us, like we made a nice couple or something. Maybe we did.

"Miss you, too," I said.

You can't forget to say stuff like that to people, like I always used to. Besides, now I really meant it.

Nanny and Grampop came to the bus station to pick me up, and they brought Bill. He was so big. Huge. He was five now, and almost too big for Nanny and Grampop to pick up.

He came running at me and hugged me around my knees and said, "Hi, Thynnie, hi, Thynnie hi." He was strong, too.

Bill said "hi" now. He said a few things now, not just "Thynnie."

Nanny said he'd learned all kinds of new words. She said Bill might even surprise me that weekend, because I might even hear a new word I hadn't heard on the telephone. She said new words popped up every day now. But even if he'd never learned another word his whole life, it wouldn't have mattered to me.

Grampop came over and gave me a great big bear hug and said, "Great to see you, Cynthia. You never looked better."

It was hard to imagine that these were the same people who never even came into my hospital room in Arizona. Who wouldn't even look at me. But I knew it wasn't Nanny and Grampop who had changed. I was the one who had changed.

I waited until Bill took his afternoon nap the next day to have our talk. Because even though he wouldn't understand the words, Bill knew a lot about when people were mad and upset. I wanted to make sure he didn't hear us fighting.

I just told Nanny and Grampop straight out that I needed to talk to them about something important. That way there was no backing down.

Nanny made tea, and we sat at the dining room table.

I said, "In three years . . . when I'm eighteen . . . I'm going to try to get custody of Bill."

They looked at each other for a minute.

Then Nanny said, "How will you look after him, dear?"

"Well, Pat says we can rent a room in her house. And I'll work and go to school. And we're looking into getting him into a special school, so he'll be gone part of the day, anyway. But Pat will look after him when I'm not around."

They looked at each other again and nodded a little.

Nanny said, "That sounds fine, dear."

I guess I was so prepared for what to say, I just said it anyway. I said, "I know it's kind of weird, me fighting you for custody and all."

"There's no need for a fight," Nanny said. "If you really keep doing this well . . . we'd be happy for you to take him."

I was quiet for a minute, wondering where all that scary stuff had gone. "You would?"

Grampop said, "Oh, God, yes! When we took that kid I thought it'd be just temporary. I thought your mom would get her act together. But it doesn't look like that's gonna happen, and it's not like Bill's going to grow up and be on his own." I saw him look up at Nanny and then look away, like he was ashamed. I could tell she was giving him that look. Like he was being way too honest. His voice got softer. "Anyway, you've earned a lot of trust back this year. I hope you really do keep it up. You're doing something even your mom can't seem to do."

Then we were all quiet for a while, because it was hard, talking about my mom. It's like we all knew she was pretty much a lost cause, and we all felt bad about it, but there was nothing we could do. Every time her name came up, there was this moment of silence. Like she died or something. It was so sad.

"I really appreciate this," I said.

"You'll be earning it," Grampop said. And that means a lot coming from Grampop. It might not be much credit, but he doesn't give you any credit unless you really deserve it.

Then he left to take a nap, and Nanny and I sat at the table together for a while longer.

Nanny said, "Remember when you sent that letter apologizing for everything you did?"

"Yeah. Be kind of hard to forget."

"I've been feeling bad ever since then. And now I know why. Because *I* owed *you* an apology, too. For just leaving you in that house on your own with her. I tried to talk Grampop into taking you, too. But he didn't even want to take Bill. He never wanted any more kids. He said we paid our dues already on kids. But at least I could've told you how hard I tried. But I didn't, and I don't know why not. It's like I had to pretend you were fine there on your own or I wouldn't have been able to do it." A long silence. I didn't know if I was supposed to say something or not.

Nobody in my family had ever made amends to *me*. "Anyway. I'm sorry."

"Thanks," I said. "I appreciate your saying that." More silence. It was reminding me why my family never talks about things. Because when we do, it feels so awkward and strange. "I'm going to go sit in the bedroom," I said. "I'll be careful not to wake Bill." I think she knew I was really saying, I'm going to go look at Bill while he sleeps. I think she understood.

Nanny and Grampop had set up a rollaway bed for me in Bill's room, and I sat down on it. Just sat and watched Bill sleep. He was faced away, so I was just seeing the back of his hair, all mussy and dark. A bunch of afternoon light came in through the window and fell over the back of his head, like he was the lightest thing in the world.

I don't know how long I sat there staring at him. Might have been just a few minutes, or maybe even an hour. I wasn't keeping track.

Then he woke up and rolled over, and he looked so happy to see me.

"Thynnie, hi. Hi, Thynnie. Morning. Thynnie, morning."

It wasn't morning, exactly, but I knew what he meant. He meant he woke up.

He got out of bed and ran over to me and I picked him up. He was heavy, but I picked him up anyway. I just did. And I danced him around and around the room, and I told him all about how it was going to be, in three years, when he came to live with me. It made him really happy. Maybe he didn't understand all the words, but he knew I was happy, so he got happy, too. He dropped his head back and threw his arms out wide like he was flying. The look on his face was just the greatest thing. I knew that for the next three years, I'd never forget it. No matter how long it seemed or how tough it got, for the next three years I would never once forget that smile.